T0267483

The DONUT PRINCE

of NEW YORK

a novel by ALLEN ZADOFF

HOLIDAY HOUSE • NEW YORK

HOLIDAY HOUSE is registered in the U.S. Patent and Trademark Office.

Printed and bound in September 2024 at Sheridan, Chelsea, MI, USA.

www.holidayhouse.com

First Edition

10 9 8 7 6 5 4 3 2 1

Library of Congress Cataloging-in-Publication Data is available.

ISBN: 978-0-8234-5663-5 (hardcover)

"Have a belief in yourself that is bigger than anyone's disbelief."

—August Wilson

CHAPTER ONE:

I DON'T BELIEVE IT

I'm at the Donut Prince on Eighth Avenue in Times Square, its famous neon crown glowing like a beacon of sugary hope. It's the end of summer, the final long days of August reminding you of the summer you had—or the summer you wish you'd had. Guess which team I'm on?

Until now.

I'm sitting in the window holding a half-eaten double chocolate, more frosting on my shirt than on the donut, when this girl walks in.

She's all curves and caramel hair, laughing like she's in on a secret joke with the universe. Despite the heat outside, she's wearing a leather jacket over biker shorts, and her fingers dance across her phone's screen as she waits for her order. She loves donuts, so it's clearly a match.

I try not to stare, but every once in a while, I sneak a glance. In my head, I'm already up at the counter.

I noticed you ordered the strawberry rhubarb jelly–filled. Bold move. They are the Hamlet of donuts: complex, moody, yet worth the emotional investment. Like me.

She laughs and her eyes sparkle.

I tell her I'm going to be a famous playwright someday, and she tells me she loves theater. And just like that, my entire life changes.

A honking cab interrupts my fantasy. I look down at the half-eaten donut, then back at her paying at the counter.

You're supposed to be a playwright, Eugene. Just say something funny.

I slip off the stool, ready to make my move, when I catch sight of my reflection in the front window—a very large teenager clutching a donut like a life preserver.

I know there are big people who love their bodies—but for whatever reason, I'm not one of them.

I try to find some inspiration in my head, a film or play where a big guy gets the girl without it being a joke—but I'm drawing a blank. There are no love stories with people who look like me.

So even if I talked to her, what good would it do?

I look at the reflection of my large body in the window with her smaller body framed behind me—and I sit back down.

A bell dings. She's going out the front door, phone in one hand, a donut bag in the other. I don't believe I'm letting the girl of my dreams walk away, but that's what happens. I watch her through the window, and I do nothing.

I take a deep breath and put my head on the counter. I'm so angry with myself, I can barely think straight.

I make a silent vow that I'm going to change. Eugene Guterman, man of action. The man who put down donuts and picked up courage.

But when I sit up, there's half a double chocolate still in my hand. What kind of monster leaves half a donut?

So I down it in two bites, promising myself it's the last one.

I stop at the counter to say goodbye.

"You ready for another, hon?"

It's my friendly donut dealer in a white cap. Sweet, nonjudgmental, and about three decades too old for me. Oh well.

"I shouldn't—" I start to say.

"—but they're the best in the city." We finish my sentence in unison.

I sigh. We have so much in common.

"One more for the road," I say. "Make it a maple-glazed."

CHAPTER TWO:

THE DREADED FRITTATA

"Eugene!!! Breakfast!" It's the shrill voice of Miriam Guterman, MD, echoing through our apartment like an ambulance siren.

I snap awake, squinting at the morning light streaming through the blinds. I'm pretty sure I was back at the Donut Prince in my dreams, only I was brave this time. I talked to that girl in the leather jacket and I got her number.

Now that I'm awake, I realize that didn't happen.

Reality rushes in. The last day of summer break has become the first day of school. So much for my summer plans.

Mom pops her head in the door without even knocking. She's perpetually wearing scrubs, and her goal seems to be to get me to wear them, too. The sooner the better.

"Privacy, Mom."

"You don't want to be late on your first day of junior year, do you?"

"I hope that's a rhetorical question."

Mom looks at me, suddenly concerned. "What's up with you today?"

"Nothing," I say quickly. "I can't wait to get this year started."

"I detect a note of sarcasm."

"More than a note. I could write a Broadway musical on the subject."

I glance at the blank notebook perched on my desk across the room. Who am I kidding? I haven't written anything all summer.

"Healthy breakfast for two, coming right up," Mom says, and she goes back to the egg white cooking facility she calls our kitchen.

I force a smile. *Healthy breakfast for two.* That's a double dig— "healthy" because I need to lose weight, and "two" instead of three because Dad left last year.

My parents met way back when Mom was in medical school at Columbia and Dad was a promising screenwriter at NYU.

Science and art. Opposites attract.

They got married, had me, then lived happily ever after. For exactly sixteen years, at which point my dad fell in love with an actress a decade younger and moved to Astoria.

He traded soaring views of Lincoln Center for the odor of Queens. That does not seem like an upgrade to me, but what do I know?

I roll out of bed and confront my dresser.

Some days it feels like clothes are my enemy. And by some, I mean every day since middle school.

I'm halfway through a wrestling match with a pair of stiff jeans when I look back at my desk. My writing notebook is sitting open, the blank pages mocking me.

I get a pang as I think about my summer dreams. Meet a girl, write a great play that will redeem my reputation at school—

I didn't do either of those things.

A lot of kids won't write, even under court order. But I spent all summer trying to create this new play. The actors are counting on me. The theater club is counting on me.

I just have to finish it. And also change my name because Eugene Guterman doesn't sound like a famous playwright's name to me. It sounds more like a roofing contractor in Long Island.

"Eugene, I made you an egg white frittata!"

Ugh. Another frittata. There hasn't been a decent breakfast pastry in this house since the Obama Administration.

"The frittata is hot and delicious," Mom shouts, elongating the word into a dramatic cry of maternal hope and desperation.

It's a good performance, but I'd still rather have a donut.

CHAPTER THREE:
JUNIOR PEAK

Mia Kim is filled with energy this morning. Maybe it's the giant iced coffee clutched between her hands. When she takes a sip, her entire head disappears behind the cup.

"Junior year!" Mia says. "We made it!"

I always pick up Mia on Seventy-First Street so we can walk the rest of the way to school together. It's a tradition with us—we've done it every day since we bonded the first month of middle school. The playwright and the computer geek, science and art, just like my parents. Unlike my parents, we became friends and stayed that way.

"You're not psyched about school," Mia says.

"How can you tell?"

"Your face. You had the same expression when they closed Broadway during Covid."

"My mom cooked another egg white frittata. I think *frittata* is Italian for 'depression.'"

Mia laughs too loud, and I suddenly realize something is different about her.

"Hang on—you're glowing."

"I'm upbeat."

"Since when? What happened to my brilliant, depressed partner in crime?"

"That's the old me," she says. "Welcome to the new me."

She spins and strikes a pose, kicking up one foot like she's in a try-on haul.

Did she cut her hair? No, that's not it. Get new glasses? Nope, those look the same. Then it hits me—she's not wearing her usual hoodie and sweatpants.

"You got an extreme makeover," I say.

"Not extreme. I just bought some decent clothes and colored my hair."

"But why? You never cared about that stuff before."

"We have to peak this year. How can we have a senior slide if we don't have a junior peak?"

"A peak? That sounds like a lot of work."

The truth is I tried to peak sophomore year, but I had the weight-gain thing, the dad-leaving thing, and the embarrassing-play-everyone-hated thing. I guess my peak became a valley.

"I don't want to be the same person I was the last two years," she says adamantly.

"You mean my best friend and trusted advisor?"

"I mean the nerdy girl who's too afraid to take a risk, then falls asleep watching K-dramas every night. Do you know how many times I've seen *Extraordinary Attorney Woo*?"

"I don't know what that is."

"Eugene!"

"I'm not into streaming. I'm a theater person."

"So am I," she says defensively.

Mia helped upgrade our theater's lighting console last year and she does a lot of technical work in our black-box space. That doesn't exactly qualify her as a theater person in my eyes. More like a theater appreciator. But I'm not complaining.

"Cornell Tech hit me hard this summer," Mia says. She lowers her voice and leans in, a glimmer in her eyes. "I know what I want to do for my capstone project."

"Capstone? That's senior year!"

"Not necessarily. Some kids start junior year. I might even try for early admission."

"You said junior peak, senior slide. This sound more like a junior launch pad."

"You haven't even heard the idea yet," she says. "Get this: I'm going to create a start-up for a new kind of social media. ASM. Authentic Social Media."

"So that's what's going on."

My heart sinks. I don't want to lose my friend to some tech dream, no matter how cool it sounds.

"How about a little encouragement?" she says. "You have Broadway dreams and I have start-up dreams. We're in this together, right?"

I nod tentatively.

"So how's the big play coming?" Mia asks.

I think about the blank pages in my notebook.

"Could be bigger," I say.

"The theater club is super excited. They've been texting about it nonstop."

"I'm taking my time on this one. You remember what happened last year."

Our drama club did a one-act play festival, and my one act lasted an hour and a half. The reviewer for the school paper said I made one act feel like five. I thought it was a compliment until I read the rest of the review.

"What's the new play about?" Mia asks.

Sweat breaks out on my forehead. How do you talk about a play you haven't started yet?

"It's a tragic retelling of Jack and Jill."

"The nursery rhyme?"

"Yeah, but my version's cool. After a personal tragedy on the hill, Jill transforms herself, hitting the gym, getting buff, then returning to the village to seek revenge and retrieve her pail. It's called *Jacked Jill.*"

She looks confused, so I strike a weight lifter pose.

"*Jacked* Jill. Get it? Because Jill's buff."

Mia is silent. I don't think it's the stunned silence of someone who just heard the greatest idea ever.

"You always do adaptations," she says.

"Excuse me—I do mashups."

She shrugs. "Why don't you just write about your life?"

"Why would I do that? There's nothing interesting about my life."

"I disagree," she says.

"And I disagree with your disagreement."

We turn the corner and I see our school in the distance, the sidewalk out front cluttered with students.

"We're both going to do big things this year," Mia says.

"I always do big things," I say, gesturing to my stomach. "I can't help it."

"I'm serious."

"Okay, you'll change the tech world and I'll change the theater world. We'll both be junior-year trailblazers."

Her face broadens into a smile. "That's what I'm talking about!"

She holds out her hand for a pinkie swear, and I hesitate.

I want to be the kind of person Mia is talking about. Excited, optimistic, passionate. I just don't want to fail again.

Mia keeps her pinkie extended, seemingly unaware of how uncool a pinkie swear is.

Our pinkies meet in midair. It's not exactly Arthur pulling the sword from the stone in Camelot, but it feels like something important is happening.

"This is going to be our year, Eugene," she says, her voice low and filled with determination.

"Our year," I repeat.

And we cross the street together and head into school.

CHAPTER FOUR:
MEET THE MUSE

"You're not going to believe what's happening!" Ishaan sprints down the hall like he's been waiting for us, violin case strapped across his back, limbs flailing and face beaming with excitement. He races past Mia and plants himself across from me.

"There's a new girl," he says breathlessly. "A junior like us. Just transferred."

Mia raises an eyebrow. "A new junior. I'm surprised that didn't make the *Times* this morning."

"What does it have to do with me?" I ask Ishaan.

"She's your type," Ishaan says.

"I'm sick of you objectifying women," Mia says.

"For your information, I'm not objectifying. I'm appreciating a stranger from a distance."

"That's the definition of *objectify*, Ishaan."

"It's also the definition of *attraction*, Mia."

"Kids, play nicely together," I say.

We're only a minute into junior year and my best friends are already engaging in stage combat. I was hoping for a little détente this year, but I can see it was wishful thinking.

"I feel bad for this girl," I say. "Sucks to be new your junior year. No friends, having to start all over again."

"You're missing the point," Ishaan says, then he looks at Mia. "Could you excuse us? My associate and I need to partake in guy talk, and you have sensitive ears."

"I understand guy talk," Mia protests.

"You claim to understand, but you get preachy," he says.

Wabash Simpson passes by. He's the president of the drama club, renowned for his extravagant headwear collection. Today he's wearing a cowboy hat tied off with a red bandana. I'm sure they wouldn't even blink an eye in Texas, but this is the Upper West Side of Manhattan.

"The Three Musketeers," Wabash says when he sees us. "All for one—"

"And one for all," we say in unison. It's geeky, and we know it's geeky, but Wabash eats it up.

He nods to Ishaan, bows grandly to Mia, then looks at me curiously.

"Have you spurned technological communication?" he asks me.

I look away and clear my throat. I've been avoiding his texts and DMs for a month. He keeps asking about my new play and I don't know what to tell him.

"Busy," I say.

"Busy writing?"

"You know it."

"Can't wait to see some pages," he says. "We have to dive into casting before the drama department snatches up all the talent for their fall extrava-BLAND-za."

After my one-act play ran a little long last year, Wabash said the

13

one-act format may have been too limiting, and he offered me a production slot of my own.

Fall play. Full support of our school's large and dedicated theater club. Plus, he wants to stick it to the theater department, which he considers our competition.

"Speaking of talent," Wabash says, turning to Mia and Ishaan. "Can we count on you to run the light board again this year, Mia?"

"I'm all over that board," she says.

"And you, Ishaan—set crew?"

"For sure," Ishaan says.

"With that, I bid you adieu," Wabash says. "See you at club!"

As soon as he's gone, Ishaan turns to me. "So the play's going well?"

"Really well."

That's the third time I've lied this morning. I don't have the heart to admit I wasted an entire summer.

"I have to get to homeroom," Mia says. "Eugene, I'll catch you later. Ishaan—don't get him in trouble."

"Don't worry, Mom," he says.

Mia frowns and heads off. Ishaan waits for her to get out of earshot, then looks back at me curiously.

"Did she change her hair?"

"More than her hair," I say. "Cornell Tech changed her whole vibe. She's got start-up fever."

"She's a Stemmy now?"

"I think she always was. She's just growing into it."

"Good for her," he says. "So about the new girl—"

"Why are you so excited about her?" I ask.

14

"I'm excited about girls in general," Ishaan says, and adjusts his violin case across his back. "But this one's not for me. She's your type."

"How can you know my type if I don't know my type?"

"Because I'm your best friend."

"If this girl's so special, why don't you try to date her?"

"I already have someone in mind." His face turns red as he leans in, beckoning me closer. "Jazmin Cole," he whispers.

"The cheerleader?"

He nods.

"She's a senior. And she's—"

"Out of my league?" he asks.

"I didn't say that." But I have to admit it's what I was thinking.

"We all got dreams," Ishaan says with a shrug. "Besides, it's our junior year. We have to peak."

I shake my head. "Not you, too. Mia and I already had this discussion."

"Junior peak, senior slide. Everyone knows."

"That is not a thing," I say.

"Look out," Ishaan says, subtly pointing down the hall.

A group of football bros is coming toward us, laughing and play-fighting, drawing the attention of the crowd. I move a little closer to the wall and lower my voice. I'm already a target because of my weight—I don't need to draw any extra attention.

"Hope you're enjoying our greenroom," Ishaan calls out, and the football players glance over, confused.

"Don't antagonize them," I whisper.

The football players are Upper West High royalty—they get the bulk of the attention and funding while the theater department gets drained of resources. Last year the school turned the greenroom where we hang out during shows into an extended locker room. That started a war between theater people and the football team.

But the football team is so self-involved, I'm not sure they even know we're at war.

"It was nice to have a jock-free summer," I say.

"They still giving you trouble?"

"A couple of them. Only when they catch me alone and feel like poking my stomach."

I don't know a ton of seniors, but everyone knows these guys. Harry Habib, captain of the football team and the best athlete in our school. He's with a couple of his bros—Dillon, who is the size of a mountain and teased me my freshman year and made my list of Most Hated Upperclassmen, and Langford, who's about six foot two of pure muscle. Langford has never teased me himself, but he didn't stop Dillon from doing it, so he also made my list.

The jocks pass by without incident and I breathe a sigh of relief.

"Back to more important things, like theater and women," Ishaan says. "Here's a thought—maybe this new girl could be the muse for your play!"

"I don't need a muse. Plus, that's like an outdated, sexist concept."

"Women have muses, too. Cardi B has Offset."

"I have no idea who those people are."

"Dude—we need girlfriends. I can't have another sexless year. It's bad for my acne. And it's bad for your development as a dramatist. How can you write about love if you've never experienced it?"

"My writing is fine."

"Really? 'Cause I haven't read anything all summer."

I stare at my feet, embarrassed.

"Your one-act play last year was the best thing I ever saw," Ishaan says.

"Half the audience fell asleep," I remind him. "And the school reviewer hated it."

"What does that reviewer know?"

"His dad is the theater critic for the *New York Times*. Anyway, it's my own fault. I shouldn't have tried to cram a whole Shakespeare adaptation into one act."

"You retold *Twelfth Night* as a supernatural horror story. What was it called again?"

"*Friday the Thirteenth Night.*"

"Evil twins. Brilliant."

"You're the only one who thought that. You and Mia."

"In other words, the two people who know you best in the world. Wabash loved it, too. He gave you your own production slot."

"I think it's a pity production."

The warning bell rings.

"And so it begins," Ishaan says, heaving his backpack onto one shoulder. "Your muse's name is Daisy Luna. Don't forget."

He pulls a pack of mints from his pocket and extends them my way. Ishaan's been carrying mints since freshman year, just in case he has to kiss a girl on short notice.

"I don't need those," I say.

Truth is, neither does he. I think that pack of mints is three years old now.

"Take your time when you meet her," Ishaan says. "You tend to get flustered around women."

"Since when?"

"Since birth."

"I've gotta get to homeroom," I say, and I start down the hall.

"You're going to love Daisy!" Ishaan shouts after me.

CHAPTER FIVE:

THE RETURN OF THE DONUT PRINCESS

I appreciate Ishaan's enthusiasm, but I've never been great with women, and to be honest, they've never been great with me. Everyone's talking about body positivity, but nobody's been positive about my body. I guess I've got a swipe right kind of mind and a swipe left kind of body. I know how to make girls laugh, but they laugh me right into the friend zone. Despite the name, it's not all that friendly there.

So as the day rolls on, I forget all about Daisy Luna, Ishaan's mysterious stranger. Instead, I focus on a more immediate threat. My nemesis, Coach Kyle.

Othello had Iago. Elphaba had Galinda. I have an Australian bro who wears super-tight shorts and gave me the only C of my high school career.

One day last year, I skipped gym so I could go to the library and read a Suzan-Lori Parks play. That day, Coach Kyle caught me and glared like I'd broken a sacred oath. "You think you can dodge responsibility? You think you can dodge life?" he barked. All because I dodged gym.

Gym is rough on kids like me. Just the idea of changing in the locker room is enough to give me panic perspiration.

But Coach Kyle was unmoved by my plea for mercy. He brought the Aussie fist of justice down and gave me a C.

My mom had a fit. To her, the future of medical school hung in the balance. I begged Coach Kyle to change the grade, offered to make up the class or do anything that would restore my 4.0 average, but he wouldn't budge. He called it tough love.

I called it the kind of rage-filled vengeance Hugh Jackman exhibited in the Wolverine movies.

Which brings us up to date. First day of school, and I was not looking forward to seeing Coach Kyle—or the locker room—again. But it's not like I have a choice. When third period arrives, I walk onto the field located on the roof of our school wearing my favorite gym uniform—a full tracksuit. It's hot in New York today, but not hot enough for me to reveal my legs in shorts.

I look across the line of students, a selection of juniors and seniors who are hungrily eyeing each other like they haven't seen the opposite sex before. Or the same sex. Or any sex.

Me and my tracksuit drift to the back of the crowd as I scan for friendly faces. I forgot to text Ishaan and Mia to see if they were in this class, and now I'm alone and dressed like a character from *The Sopranos*. That makes it tough to fade into the background, but I do my best.

Coach Kyle bursts onto the field, a whirlwind of tanned muscle, mini-shorts, and a grin that's one part charm, two parts arrogance. His white T-shirt clings to his biceps as he struts around, clapping kids on the back, asking about their summers like he's hosting a beach party.

I suddenly hear a girl's voice nearby.

"I saw those shorts at babyGap last week. They were in the small pants/big ego section," she says.

I turn too quickly, tripping on my oversized tracksuit and just barely catching myself. I look up to find a familiar-looking girl standing next to me. Caramel hair, brown skin, huge eyes—

"What's up, Donut Prince?" she asks with a smile.

"You're the girl from—"

"I'm Daisy," she says. "I've seen you around. Obviously we both have good taste in baked goods."

I can't believe what I'm hearing. It's my dream girl from the Donut Prince, and we're actually talking.

"I'm Eugene," I say. "And I think their donuts are fried, not baked."

"Fried, baked, shot out of a cannon. If it's food, I'm in." She must see the amazement on my face, because she adds: "I'm not obsessed. I do some food and travel videos online."

"You're an influencer?"

"Micro-influencer. But I've got eleven followers who love my work."

"Soon to be a dozen," I say.

The conversation is flowing, just like in my fantasy.

"Do you believe in second chances, Daisy?"

"I hope so. I'm kind of living one."

"Oh yeah? What's the story?"

"We moved from Philly during the summer. Fresh start and all that," Daisy says, glancing away.

"Must have been serious to move away from Philly cheesesteak."

"We have some killer barbacoa, too—lamb tacos. But I also miss the cheesesteak. And yeah, I've got some history there."

"If you're running from cheesesteak, I should probably be running from donuts. Or just running for exercise."

She laughs. "All things in moderation, right?"

"I don't really know how to do that."

"Me neither," she says with a wink. "Which is why it's good to have a fresh start this year."

I steal another look at her. I'm trying not to do the objectification thing Mia is always talking about, but Daisy looks even better up close. Her face is glowing in the sunlight, and her body is amazing, swells and curves in all the right places.

Coach Kyle blows his whistle, snapping me out of my reverie.

"I am not looking forward to this," I say with a sigh.

"Not a gym rat?"

"Jocks and theater people don't mix in our school."

"I like theater," Daisy says.

I like theater. Are there three more beautiful words in the English language?

Our conversation is cut short by Coach shouting for the guys to line up on one side of the field, and the girls on the other.

"See you around, Donut Prince."

I barely have time to wave goodbye as Daisy jogs to the other side of the field.

I reluctantly get in line with a bunch of guys way more fit than me, all of whom look excited to be here. What type of human is excited about phys ed? It's baffling to me.

I feel an elbow in my ribs. It's Ishaan, long skinny legs sticking out the bottom of his gym shorts. I've never been so grateful to see a familiar face.

"You talked to her!" he says excitedly.

"You were watching us?"

"I was ready to swoop in as your wingman, but my services were not required. So Daisy Luna—what did you think?"

"She likes theater."

Ishaan grins. "I'm always right. It's uncanny."

"She's interesting," I say, downplaying it. "But I can't go crazy for some girl I just met."

"Why not?"

"Because then I would be you."

"Easy on your best friend, huh? I'm trying to change your life here."

"Sorry. These track pants are so tight they're cutting off the blood supply to my colon. Anyway, our conversation lasted like sixty seconds."

"You made her laugh," he says, like I just invented cold fusion. "If you make them laugh, you're fifty percent there."

"What's the other fifty percent?"

"Looks, money, athletic prowess, popularity."

"So you're saying I'm screwed."

"I'm saying it's a long climb to a hundred percent. But you're off to a great start."

Coach Kyle blows a double tap on his whistle and launches into his first of what is sure to be many motivational speeches of the year.

"Transformation," he says in a thick Australian accent. "The tadpole becomes the frog, the caterpillar becomes the butterfly, the weak become the strong. It is through transformation and hard work that we become who we were meant to be."

"What is he talking about?" Ishaan asks.

I look across the baffled faces of the kids around me. Then I see Daisy in line on the other side of the field, and my legs go weak.

"Transformation takes willpower," Coach Kyle says. "It takes focus. It takes commitment. You will need all three as we begin our new wellness campaign this year."

"Wellness campaign?" Ishaan whispers.

"It sounds unhealthy," I say.

"We'll begin with a physical assessment," Coach says, "then we'll separate you into teams, and you'll spend the semester working to improve your conditioning. Today you are helpless tadpoles, but soon you will be mighty frogs."

"Can't we just play dodgeball?" a kid at the end of the row asks.

That kid should receive an award for courage.

"Dodgeball is a distraction," Coach Kyle says, and makes direct eye contact with me. "The name of the game this year is transformation!"

The class explodes with applause, but my hands are firmly down by my sides. "Transformation" sounds a lot like a diet, and I get enough pressure about that at home.

Suddenly Harry Habib, captain of the football team, appears, slow jogging onto the field with all the authority of the varsity elite. I've heard about being fashionably late to parties, but I didn't know it applied to gym class, too. My jaw clenches as Harry runs his fingers through his long hair like a male model, and the girls start to giggle nervously.

"Is Harry in our class this semester?" Ishaan groans. "That's gonna make it tough on us plebes."

" 'Sup, Coach?" Harry says, clapping his hands in front of his chin and bowing his head as if he's deeply remorseful. "Did you give them the transformation speech yet?"

"You're late," Coach says sternly, but his frown quickly transforms into a gaping smile.

"Bro!" Harry says.

"Long live the king!" Coach says, greeting Harry with a bear hug followed by a complex handshake, grunting, and pounding each other's backs while Harry's football bros Dillon and Langford whoop it up from the class ranks. If testosterone had an odor, the city of New York would be collectively holding its nose right now.

I sneak a glance at Daisy, secretly hoping she's immune to jocks and their powerful pheromones.

No such luck. She's looking at Harry, just like everyone else.

"Grab you a piece of line so we can get the assessment going," Coach says.

Harry glances from the line of girls on one side of the field to the line of guys on the other. Then he does the unimaginable. He jogs directly into the middle of the girls, accompanied by peals of laughter.

"Coach told me to line up," Harry says, feigning innocence, "and this line smells a lot better than the other one." The giggles only get louder.

"Dear God," Ishaan says. "Let me learn from this legend among men."

"I think I threw up a little in my mouth," I say.

Just then, a voice booms across the field, "I challenge Harry!"

Everyone turns to see who spoke. Daisy is standing in the center of the field, smiling defiantly and pointing to Harry. I gasp in shock.

"If you can beat me in a race around the track, you win a prize," Daisy says.

"What prize?"

"My phone number."

Harry grins and my guts clench.

"Hey, Coach," Harry says. "You mind if I show the new girl what's up? From a fitness standpoint?"

Coach sighs, but he doesn't object.

Harry steps forward and looks at Daisy. "You really think you can beat me?"

"Not think. *Know*," Daisy says.

"You're on, new girl!" Harry says.

I look to Ishaan for moral support, but he's staring in awe at Harry's antics.

The entire class cheers as Harry and Daisy take their marks. Coach Kyle blows his whistle, and they're off, their strides seemingly in sync as they round the track. Harry soon pulls ahead, but Daisy keeps up, a ferocious determination on her face.

Suddenly Harry puts it into overdrive and laps her in the last seconds.

The crowd goes wild as he crosses the finish line, with a breathless Daisy making it a few seconds later.

But Daisy isn't discouraged. Instead, she looks satisfied with her performance.

"That was close," she says, smiling at Harry.

"For a while," he says. "I'll give you credit. I had to hustle a little out there."

"I'm out of practice," she says. "Maybe I'll get you next time."

Harry smiles and claps her on the back. "Good try. Now let's see that number."

He pulls out his phone and passes it to her.

How did he get a friggin' phone onto the field in gym class?

Daisy laughs and types in her number.

"What do I do?" I ask Ishaan, feeling more desperate with each passing second. "I can't out-Harry Harry."

Ishaan bites at his lower lip. He's as clueless as I am.

☉ ☉ ☉

I was right to worry. Coach separates us into groups with one student in each group selected to record our scores. A number of stations are set up around the field. Push-ups, pull-ups, timed run, burpees—it's a bucket list of my least favorite activities on earth, performed spitting distance from some of the best athletes in our school.

I reluctantly take my place on the starting line with four other students, preparing to run the wind sprint. I'm going to need more than wind to make it through this. I'm going to need a freak tornado to pick me up and deposit me at the finish line.

I look over at Daisy stretching on the other side of the field. I'm feeling desperate after what I just saw between Daisy and Harry. As I crouch down, something shifts inside me. My fear is replaced with a sudden surge of confidence. Maybe transformation is possible, just like Coach said. What did he tell us was required? Commitment—

I'm trying to remember the rest when the whistle blows, and I'm out of time. I push off, ready to find my inner athlete and reveal him to the world. But before I know it, my back leg contacts my front leg, and my face contacts the grass as I go down in a sprawl. I smell the dirt in my nose and hear the laughter of kids in the distance. I roll over on my back just in time to watch the race end without me.

"Man down!" Langford shouts. He's laughing at me, like the rest of Harry's guys.

"Thar she blows!" his buddy Dillon calls out, hands on his 'fro as he feigns horror.

"That's enough," Coach says, and punctuates it with a quick blast on his whistle.

Coach comes over to check on me. The look of pity on his face is too much, and I wave him off, rolling over and slowly getting to all fours before heaving myself up.

I don't dare look at Daisy. I don't want to see her reaction to what just happened.

I slink to the sidelines, trying not to draw too much attention. Ishaan appears a second later.

"I think I blew it," I say.

Ishaan claps me on the back. "Don't worry about it. Maybe she didn't see you fall."

"Really? They could see it from the International Space Station."

"It wasn't so bad."

I want to believe him, but I know he's just trying to make me feel better.

The rest of class passes in a slow-motion blur. I fail at everything I try, coming in last or near last in every assessment. By the time Coach Kyle blows the final whistle, I'm spent. It's all I can do to stay on my feet.

"Decent first day," Coach says, eyes sweeping over us. When he reaches me, his gaze lingers for an uncomfortable beat. "I know you're all doing your best, but some of us need to dig deeper."

His words are like a final kick to a man who's already down. As I start to leave the field, I glance at Daisy. I want to talk to her again, but I'm too embarrassed.

I turn in the opposite direction and bump right into Harry.

"Better luck next time, big guy," he says with a grin.

"Maybe I'll challenge you to a race," I say, anger momentarily overcoming my insecurities.

Harry's smirk widens. "Oh yeah? Can't wait to see it, bro."

He laughs and walks away, his words echoing in my head. I've got nothing to prove to him, which makes me all the more angry—for talking to him, for taking the bait, for feeling like a fat kid in a world of thin.

CHAPTER SIX:

IT'S CALLED GRAVITY

I'm famished after gym class and I rush into the cafeteria, scanning the choices like a hero looking for a weapon. I know I should choose a healthy snack like fruit or a protein bar, but the package of powdered donuts calls to me. Sorry, Miriam Guterman, MD. The stomach wants what it wants.

I sneak a sleeve of donuts into my backpack and head out of school.

I sit against my favorite wall outside, away from other people and my problems. I look at the pack of six mini-donuts, each one a mini-vacation for my mouth. Donuts are amazing things. One bite has the power to turn a bad day into a good day.

"Why'd you take off after gym?" Ishaan asks, catching me mid-bite.

"You saw what happened up there."

"It's called gravity. Anyone can slip."

"When a fat person slips, it turns gravity into comedy. Even Aristotle knew that."

Ishaan looks momentarily confused. "Nobody laughed. Except a couple of jock idiots."

"I hope those jocks didn't take a video. I don't need to go viral."

I dig into another donut, the white powder forming a cloud as I talk. "The one day I wanted to look good in front of a girl—"

Mia appears from around the corner. So much for eating in peace.

She rushes over, ignoring the fact I'm in mid-conversation and mid-snack.

"I had a brainstorm," Mia says. "My new start-up—I'm going to call it Anti-Social."

"Sounds right up my alley," I say, polishing off another bite. Three mini-donuts down, three to go.

"What are we talking about?" Ishaan asks.

"Mia has a new start-up idea. Remember I mentioned it to you?"

"I'm building a social media site for people who hate social media," she says.

"If they hate it, why would they come to your site?" Ishaan asks.

Mia pauses for a moment, processing Ishaan's comment. Just when I think she's stumped, she comes up with an answer.

"People still want to share online," Mia says. "But without the humble bragging and the peer pressure and bullying. They don't hate social media; they hate the existing social media. My site will be real. ASM. Authentic Social Media."

Touché, Mia.

"Nobody wants real," Ishaan says. "We want fantasy."

I think about Daisy Luna. She's a fantasy to me right now, but I'd like her to be a reality. I just have to figure out how to make that happen.

"I agree with Mia," I say. "Real is better."

Ishaan frowns at me.

"Social media's bad for us," Mia says. "I've had FOMO since fifth grade, all because of Snap."

"Maybe your life is boring," Ishaan says. "And social media made that obvious."

"Or maybe," she says, glancing at me, "the posers and filters make you think your body isn't okay when it really is."

"My body's outstanding," Ishaan says as he strikes an unimpressive weight lifter pose.

Ishaan glances across the street where Jazmin Cole and some friends from the dance team are heading back toward school. Jazmin's long braids bounce against her shoulders as she walks.

"I know what would make my life better," Ishaan says with a sigh.

"Mine, too," I say, thinking of Daisy. "Unfortunately, I dynamited the bridge earlier."

Mia stops abruptly, taking in my nearly empty donut snack. "What's up with you?"

"I met Daisy Luna," I say.

"That girl Ishaan was drooling over?"

"That's the one. And it did not go well."

"Correction," Ishaan says. "Boy met girl, boy and girl made each other laugh, boy was off to a good start until girl saw Harry Habib—"

"So that's that." Mia cuts him off, her voice almost gleeful.

Ishaan raises an eyebrow. "Slow down. You don't meet the girl of your dreams and give up that easily."

"Girl of his dreams?" Mia says. "You've known her for fifteen seconds."

I hesitate, embarrassed to admit I'm crushing on someone in front of Mia. She's my best friend, but we don't discuss romantic stuff much. Or ever.

"I just met her," I say, "but I kind of—I already know—I like her—"

"He's stammering," Ishaan says.

"I haven't seen you at a loss for words since the drama department did *Seussical* last year," Mia says.

"Well, that was a travesty," I say. "But this Daisy girl is...kind of amazing."

"Amazing yet she's named after a droopy flower," Mia says.

"What's with the negativity?" Ishaan asks.

"You two are girl crazy, and it's gross."

"You're start-up crazy. Is that any better?"

"I'm trying to change the world," Mia says. "What are you doing?"

"I'm trying to get my V-card punched."

"I'm guessing *V* does not stand for 'violin' in that sentence," I say.

Mia kneels down next to me, her tone softening.

"What do you really know about her?" Mia asks.

"She told me a few things," I say. "Like she just moved here from Philly. And she likes theater."

"Why'd she move?"

I shrug.

"So she's mysterious," Ishaan says. "Mystery meets hotness meets a love of the dramatic arts. She's perfect for him, Mia."

"I totally embarrassed myself during gym," I say, taking a bite of donut. "And then there's Harry—"

"Temporary setback," Ishaan says. "Look, you're not going to outrun or outjump Harry, but you have something that he doesn't have."

"What's that?"

"You've got words. The pen is mightier than the jock."

"But the jock has a six-pack."

"When Daisy sees your new play, she'll forget about Harry and fall in love with you."

Ishaan's right! There's just one little problem.

"My new play?"

I let the donut fall back into the bag, my mind whirling. Scenes from my unwritten play flash through my mind.

"I have to tell you something," I say. "There's a reason you haven't read the new play. It's because I haven't written it yet."

"You mean you haven't finished it," Mia says.

"I haven't started it."

"Dude!" Ishaan says.

"No!" Mia adds.

The truth has rendered my friends monosyllabic. I knew it was a mistake.

"Do you have writer's block?" Mia asks, gently putting a hand on my forearm.

"I have everything block," I say. "The actors are waiting. Wabash is waiting. Everyone's expecting something great. It's so much pressure."

"You're great with pressure," Ishaan says.

"I'm terrible with pressure! I had to go to the bathroom nine times before the festival last year, and that was just one act. Three acts could knock out the plumbing in the entire building."

"We can fix this," Ishaan says, nudging Mia.

"Sure," she says. "We'll figure it out together."

I look at them desperately. "How? The drama club is meeting this week. Everyone's waiting—"

"No worries. You work on the play and I'll stall Wabash," Ishaan says.

"Really?"

"You're a fast writer," Mia says. "And a natural."

"And funny," Ishaan says.

I look from one to the other, a smile spreading across my face. "You guys are the best," I say. "Seriously."

"Then it's a done deal," Ishaan says. "Playwriting success awaits."

"Meanwhile, I'll investigate the new girl," Mia says, her expression determined.

"Hang on—*investigate* is a strong word," I say.

"We have to make sure she's good enough for you," Mia says. "That's what friends do for each other."

I polish off the last donut, standing and crumpling the plastic into a ball.

"All you gotta do is write the play," Ishaan says, slipping his arm around my shoulder for moral support. "And do it fast."

CHAPTER SEVEN:

I'LL BE THE HERO

I'm cutting through the park on my way home from school when I hear a familiar voice calling.

"Yo, it's my man Eugene!" Manny Cruz, one of the great playwrights of his generation, smiles and waves me over.

Manny's seated on his usual bench where the paths intersect, wearing his all-season uniform of a jean jacket and a black turtleneck. Manny looks like the famous playwright he is, but he talks like a street fighter from the Bronx. As tough as he is, his little dog Oso is even tougher. Right now the heavyset little canine naps at his feet.

"What's up?" Manny asks.

"My blood pressure," I say, thinking about everything that's gone on at school today.

"You're a little young for hypertension," Manny says.

"Getting an early start."

I give Oso a pat and join Manny on the bench. The sun sets over Central Park, casting the sky in an orange glow.

"How's Oso doing?" I ask, admiring the pup's brown fur and stubby tail.

"Mean as a rattlesnake," Manny replies fondly. "How are things at home?"

"It's like WeightWatchers prison, and my mom is the warden."

"Family can be tough. That's why they've written plays about it for a couple millennia."

"Speaking of plays, I need to write one."

"Writing contest?"

"No, a girl." I blush.

Manny laughs. "Another classic theme. Have you met her yet?"

I slump. "Met her, made a fool out of myself, now I gotta undo what I did."

Manny shrugs. "Adversity. That's how all great love stories begin."

"No offense, Manny, but I don't know any great love stories about overweight guys. The thing with this girl—another guy kind of beat me to the punch. And I crashed and burned."

"So you showed her your vulnerable side. Next time, show her another side," Manny says.

"Landscape instead of portrait?"

Manny nods. "Characters are complex, right? Lover and fool, hero and villain. Nobody's all of one and none of the other."

I sit up a little straighter in my seat. "You're saying I could be the hero?"

Manny grins. "Why not? You're a dramatist. Write yourself a different role."

The idea hits home. What if I could be like a character in one of my plays? Braver than my normal self, smarter, more daring. Donut Prince instead of Donut Eater.

A transformation, just like Coach Kyle was saying.

I jump up and give Manny a fist bump, ignoring Oso's startled yelp.

"I'm gonna write a play, and I'm gonna rewrite my life."

CHAPTER EIGHT:

SHOOT YOUR SHOT

I'm on the roof and ready for gym class early. The mostly empty field spreads out in front of me with views of the Hudson River in the distance.

After talking with Manny yesterday, I was inspired to wake up early and start a new play. I threw out *Jacked Jill* and replaced it with a funny, heartbreaking story of star-crossed lovers. *Romeo and Juliet* set in a Manhattan bakery called *What Glaze Through Yonder Window Breaks*. I didn't get much further than the title when I realized it was hard to write a play and rewrite my life at the same time. So I decided to start with my life and gradually work my way back to the play.

I glance across the field and just as I hoped, Daisy is here, warming up on the other side of the field. Time to start the rewrite.

I saunter over, pulling at my tracksuit to make sure it's hiding certain parts of me while doing my best to appear casual.

"We meet again," I say, which is what I figure a character a little more confident than me would say in this situation.

Daisy stops mid–jumping jack and looks over at me, a curious smile on her face.

"You're here early," she says. "And nice tracksuit."

"It's a look, right?" I say, pulling at my suit. I was hoping to exude confidence, but my voice sounds strange echoing across the nearly empty field. "Why are you here?"

"I wanted to get in a little extra warmup," she says. "Just in case we have to do more fitness test stuff. That first class was brutal. And Coach Kyle—"

"I call him Australia's angriest export."

Daisy grins and drops onto her back. "Do you mind holding my feet?" she asks.

I kneel down and reach for her bright white sneakers, anchoring her as she starts to do crunches, her bare legs a few inches from my face. I realize I'm staring at her legs a little too much, and I let go. The back of Daisy's head smacks against the Astroturf and she grunts.

"Um, you have to hold them down, Donut Prince."

"Sorry, I got distracted."

"By what?" she says with a grin, and she playfully nudges my calf with her sneaker.

Sweat breaks out on my forehead as I struggle for the right thing to say.

"Did your fitness test go okay?" Daisy asks.

"Are you serious? I totally embarrassed myself."

She does a full sit-up and stops, her face in front of mine. "Embarrassed?"

"You may have noticed I'm on the larger side."

"So what?"

"Tell that to my pants."

She looks confused. Is she not seeing the same fat that I am?

I can't figure out what's going on, but it's a lot safer to change the subject. What would a heroic character say right now?

"How's junior year treating you?" I ask.

"Rough."

"Sorry to hear it."

She wipes dirt from her hands and stands up, and I reluctantly let go of her legs. "I can't afford to mess up. I'm trying to have a fresh start, and I don't need any humiliating nicknames my first week," she says.

"Did you have a humiliating nickname in Philadelphia?"

"In elementary they called me Lazy Daisy. Eye problems. I had to wear a patch for a few months until it corrected itself."

"That kind of thing will traumatize you."

"For real."

"They used to call me Huge Teen instead of Eugene."

"In elementary?"

"No, yesterday afternoon."

She laughs and leans against the goalpost. "You said you were a playwright the other day. That's unusual."

"I mean, maybe. Most people would rather be an influencer like you."

"Micro-influencer, remember? Maybe that's an exaggeration. What's smaller than micro?"

"You could be the first nano-influencer."

"I guess you have to start somewhere, right?"

"I get it. I'm starting with ten-minute plays—that run a little long. I caught the theater thing from my dad. We used to go to shows a lot before my parents got divorced."

"Hey, are you going to ask me out?" she says abruptly.

I'm shocked into silence. I stand there, trying to find the words.

"I don't mean to put you on the spot," she says, "but I'm getting friend vibes and interested guy vibes, and you're telling me about your life but you're not going for it, and it's messing with my head a little. Which direction are we headed?"

Before I can answer, a shadow falls across my face. I look up and see Harry Habib towering over me and blocking the sun.

He looks down at me disinterestedly, then over at Daisy, interestedly.

"'Sup?" Harry says to her.

"Nothing," she says quietly.

"Just wanted to say hey," he says.

"Hey."

'Sup and *Hey*. One and a half words, yet Harry has turned them into a symphony of sexual tension.

"See you around," Harry tells her.

A silent moment passes between them, and then the powerful tide of Harry Habib sweeps out just as quickly as it swept in.

"So...you guys seem to be getting along," I say.

That should get me nominated for the understatement of the year award.

Daisy slowly focuses back on me. "Not really."

"You gave him your number last class, right? Now you guys are vibing."

"I gave him my number to put him in his place."

"I don't follow."

Daisy's lips curl into a smirk, and her gaze flicks back to Harry. "I

41

thought if I gave him my number, he'd never call and I wouldn't have any problems with him."

"Like reverse psychology?"

"Something like that. And it worked. He's been on his best behavior ever since. And I haven't gotten a single text." Daisy's eyes sparkle with satisfaction.

"Maybe you should give me your number, too," I say. "To get rid of me."

"Nah," she says, her voice low and teasing. "I think I'll keep you around."

I've got a minor case of whiplash. One second, I think she's into me, then she's into Harry, and now she's into—

"Showtime," she says as kids pour onto the field for phys ed. "See you soon, Your Majesty."

And she jogs away.

⊙⊙⊙

Coach arranges us across the field for the announcement of the fitness results.

It's not as if I thought the test went well for me. I just didn't imagine how badly it could go.

The scores were tallied after our assessment and the entire class is now put into color-coded teams. Pink, green, gold, etc. Coach says each team will do their activities together this semester, and sometimes teams will compete against each other or even join forces.

Sort of like *Squid Game*, only there's no food or money.

Coach goes to great lengths to explain that the teams are based on athletic ability at the present time, and they're not meant to judge or embarrass anyone, but come on—the message is clear. This is Ishaan's pecking order come to life in the form of a color-coded Excel spreadsheet.

Daisy's name gets called early and she's placed in the top tier. I'm still waiting for my name to be called when Coach finishes and closes the list. For a giddy second, I think I've turned invisible and I can leave phys ed forever. Then I hear a whistle, and I see Coach Kyle waving me over.

I slow jog toward him to give the appearance of hustle, and I paste a big fake smile on my face. "What's up, Coach?"

"Hang out for a second. I want to talk to everyone."

Everyone? I look around and see a few kids waiting with me. There's a guy with a broken ankle who has his knee on a scooter, a short girl, Rihanna, not exactly known for her athletic prowess, and Frederick, who is famous for having long Covid—which mostly flares up on test days. I look at the assembled crew, and my mood sinks. We may excel in certain subjects, but we're not exactly the crème de la crème of the athletic community.

"I didn't hear my name called," Rihanna tells Coach.

"Me either," I say.

"What team are we on, Coach?" the broken ankle kid asks.

"You're on a special team," Coach says. "We're running a pilot program in adaptive gym."

"Adapted for what?" Frederick asks.

"For each of you. We'll take you out of the regular class—move you away from the obvious challenges of the group dynamic and put you in a more personalized fitness setting."

"Where's the setting?" I ask.

"Downstairs in the weight room."

"What happened to metamorphosis?" I ask.

"We're still doing that. It's just that you're more in the larva stage."

"And the larvae stay downstairs," I say glumly.

"We don't have to go to the main class anymore?" Rihanna asks, trying to hide her excitement.

Coach nods, and Frederick pumps his fist in silent celebration.

I look over to where Daisy stands across the field, making friends with her new group.

"What if we want to stay in the main class?" I ask, and the other kids look at me like I've lost it.

"Assistant Coach Lao will help all of you get stronger downstairs," Coach says, "then we'll bring you back to the big show upstairs and assign you to a team."

"How long will that take?" I ask.

"What's going on with you, Guterman? As I recall from last year, gym class isn't exactly your preferred mode of travel."

I glance over at Daisy again. She's with a bunch of athletic-looking students, and Harry is stretching out in the group next to hers.

I see them exchange glances. Either she's the most brilliant reverse psychologist in history, or I'm in trouble.

"I got inspired by your transformation speech," I tell Coach. "It's like a miracle."

Coach leans in so nobody will overhear us.

"You may have a new attitude, but you have the same weight problem. Why don't we work on improving your body until your enthusiasm matches your ability?"

My face burns with rage. There are a lot of things I'd like to say to Coach right now, but I'm not in the mood for a month of detention.

Coach steps back and addresses the group as a whole. "If there are no other questions, let's get the adaptive gym crew off the field so we can get things rolling here."

I slip away from the group, desperate to talk to Ishaan. I find him with a scraggly team of kids in the corner of the field.

"I'm on the gray team," he says glumly. "Is gray even a color?"

He steps closer, whispering to me. "Luckily that hot new woodwind player is on my team, so all is not lost. There's something special about a girl and an oboe," he says wistfully. "So which team did you get?"

"I got pulled out of gym."

"What?"

"It's this new thing called adaptive gym. They're going to take the broken toys downstairs and try to fix us."

"It's not like you want to be the star of gym class. Maybe it'll be easier down there."

"You're missing the point. If I'm not upstairs, I'm not with Daisy."

I point across the field where Daisy's group is warming up near Harry's group.

"She's not in any of my other classes this semester. This is the only place our paths cross."

"Farther from you, closer to him," Ishaan says. "I get it now."

"I have to seal the deal," I say. "And fast."

Coach blows his whistle for the teams to assemble in the center of the field.

"We'll find a way to fix it," Ishaan says.

"How?"

"I don't know right this second, but we're geniuses, and we'll figure it out. And if we can't, Mia can."

"Mia's busy with her start-up idea. I don't think she's going to be much use to us."

Another whistle, and Ishaan joins the gray team and heads for the center of the field. I locate the adaptive gym kids on the other side of the field, heading for the stairs to go down to the weight room. The guy with the broken ankle is slowly wheeling his scooter toward the access elevator. I imagine myself in the elevator next to him, silently descending to the darkness of the weight room.

That's when Manny's words come back to me. *Play a different role.*

Last class I fell flat on my face during the running part of the fitness test, but if I run again—and run well—I'll prove I'm fit enough to stay with the regular class. Coach is always saying he wants to see some hustle, that we should get motivated and take the initiative. So that's what I'm going to do.

Today's acting challenge: play the role of a runner.

I'm already wearing a tracksuit. I'll just act like a track and field star.

It's a far-fetched plan, but desperate times call for desperate measures

"Hey, Coach!" I shout. "Check this out!"

Heads turns as I push off from my back leg and start to run. It goes much better than it did yesterday. I feel the wind in my hair, my heart beating in my chest, the crunch of fake grass beneath my feet. In my head, I'm thinking that I'm not an adaptive gym kind of guy. It's fine for those who need it, but I should be in bright sunlight, out on the field with the rest of the class. And with Daisy.

46

I pick up speed as I run for the orange cone. More people start to look my way. I notice Daisy out of the corner of my eye, but I don't let that distract me. Work first, enjoy the triumph of athletic achievement later.

I'm nearly halfway there when my balance starts to shift. I've got too much body moving too fast, and I'm not used to it. I try to slow myself down, but an object in motion tends to stay in motion, and a high-density object in motion— Well, you get the idea.

Before I realize what's happening, I've lost control of my body, and I'm hurtling across the field in an extended fall from grace. Suddenly I crash into something, going down in a sprawl, a tangle of limbs and loud grunts.

Actually, it's not something I crashed into. It's somebody.

Harry Habib.

I sit up, stunned, my head spinning. I hear a moan, and I look over at Harry. He's rolling around on the ground, screaming in pain.

Harry broke my fall, and I broke Harry.

"He sacked the quarterback!" Dillon says, and he points an accusing finger my way.

"Double H got tackled!" his buddy Langford shouts.

"I didn't tackle anybody," I say, but the words die on my lips as Coach races past me and kneels by Harry's side.

Ishaan pulls up next to me. "Do you think he's okay?" I ask.

"He's an athlete. I'm sure he'll walk it off," Ishaan says with a shrug. "Besides, how bad could it be?"

A minute later, the nurse rushes onto the field carrying a large first aid kit. After another minute, I hear the sirens roaring up West End Avenue.

47

My voice is shaky as I try to piece together what just happened. "It was an accident."

"It looked more like a premeditated attack," Ishaan says.

Harry's still on the ground moaning, and that's when I notice his arm's at a weird angle. Oh man. Harry Habib is not just in pain; he might be seriously injured.

A crowd of people swarms around us, but it's like I can only see Daisy in the crowd, her eyes wide with concern.

"What in the hell happened here?" Coach shouts over the chaos, his head on swivel until he finds me.

"I was trying to show some initiative," I tell him. I can hear the desperation in my voice. "I didn't mean for any of this to happen."

"Well, your initiative is sending Harry to the ER, Guterman. I hope you're proud," Coach snaps.

Two other coaches arrive to help Harry onto a stretcher that's magically appeared from somewhere.

"So much for walking it off," Ishaan says under his breath.

"It's more like they're rolling him off."

Daisy's gaze meets mine for just a second. Just long enough for me to see the judgment there.

The crowd parts, making way. As they cart Harry off, the field is filled with murmurs. "How could Guterman be so stupid?" "Did he do it on purpose?"

Ishaan puts his arm across my shoulders. "Dude, it's a temporary setback."

"It's looking more like a permanent problem," I say.

I glance back to where Daisy had been standing. She's no longer there. Instead, she's following the procession that's taking Harry away, a parade of concerned students. It's a scene straight out of a romantic drama, except I'm not the lead. I'm the comedic sidekick who's watching it all from the sidelines.

"Come on." Ishaan nudges me. "Let's get you out of here before the reporters from the school paper show up."

I nod, but as I start to walk off the field, Coach Kyle calls me back.

"Guterman! My office. Now."

I look to Ishaan for moral support, but there's nothing he can do for me.

The next thirty minutes are awful. Accusations, explanations, and finally, the Aussie hammer of judgment. Coach Kyle doesn't say the words *suspended* or *expelled*, but I can feel them hanging in the air like the scent of sweat in a locker room.

"Next class, you'll go directly to adaptive gym. I don't want to see you on the field for the rest of the semester," Coach says angrily. "And stay the hell away from the football team. Harry's on his way to the hospital. You're lucky his parents aren't pressing charges."

I nod, beaten.

"Dismissed," Coach finally says, and I stagger out of the office.

Ishaan is waiting for me in the hallway. He searches my face for clues. "So what's the verdict?"

"Adaptive gym, permanent touring production starring yours truly."

"Is that all?"

"That's not enough? I'm banned from the rooftop field. No phys ed, no Daisy. The jocks already hated me before this. What's going to happen now? Plus, Daisy saw the whole thing, so I didn't just tank my rep; I destroyed any chance with her."

49

Ishaan falls silent.

"No pep talk?" I ask.

"It's bad," Ishaan says.

He proceeds to sneak me out through the back of the school, avoiding football players or anyone else who knows what happened and might want payback.

CHAPTER NINE:
DAMAGE CONTROL

The news spreads through school like a Covid outbreak. Any hope I had of keeping it on the down-low is gone almost instantly. By the end of the day, everyone is talking about it, and by the next day, they're talking about me.

The whispers in the cafeteria are too much for me, so I slip out early and head for the men's room. I open the door and run directly into Harry's football bro Dillon washing his hands in the sink. I'm backing out of the room when he looks up, catching sight of me in the mirror.

"I remember you," he says through clenched teeth, and I freeze.

I flash back to freshman year when I was a scared, overweight kid trying to find his lane. Dillon was a sophomore then, and for some reason he hated me and wasn't shy about letting me know it.

"The Harry thing. Was it payback?" Dillon asks.

"It was an accident."

He shakes his head. "Either you're a traitor to the school or it was some kind of payback, but there's no way it was an accident."

He takes a menacing step toward me and I shrink away, one hand on the door handle.

"You can run," he says. "But at your weight, you won't get far."

I push through the door, sweat pooling under my arms, and hurry away, glancing behind me several times to see if I'm being chased. Eventually I slow down, but the looks of students in the hall keep me on high alert.

I've always wanted people to know who I was as a playwright, but I'm realizing there's a big difference between fame and notoriety.

I'm heading toward my next class when I get a quick glimpse of Daisy Luna in the distance talking to some friends. I'm briefly hopeful until I see her look up, catch sight of me, then ignore me and return to her conversation.

I head her way, trying to look casual. Hands in pockets, sucking in my stomach so maybe I'll look casual *and* thinner.

But what's the equivalent of "Oh crap, it's him" in a facial expression? That's how she looks when she sees me.

Her friends drift away. I can see she wants to follow them, but she pauses and, at last, turns to me.

"What's up?" she says. Her voice is so cool it sends a shiver through me.

"The other day in gym," I say, skipping over the small talk. "I tripped. That's all it was."

"Okay," she says.

"So you believe me?"

"Why not?"

"Because the whole school is saying something else."

"I didn't think you did it on purpose."

"It's still embarrassing," I say, shuffling my feet. "I shouldn't have tried to run. At my size, that's how natural disasters happen."

She smiles thinly but doesn't laugh. Is there anything worse than when a girl who used to laugh at your jokes stops laughing?

"Everything okay?" I ask.

"I don't like when you put yourself down like that."

I look away, suddenly ashamed.

"It was just a joke," I mumble. "I didn't want you to think I was a bully or something."

"Oh, it's pretty obvious you're the most sinister and hated individual at Upper West."

I stare at her in shock.

"Kidding," she says with a smile, and my blood pressure returns to a semi-normal level.

"I don't know what to do about Harry," I say.

She shrugs and it falls silent between us. I was hoping she'd have some insight, but she doesn't seem to want to get involved.

I think about what she said the other day. Am I going to ask her on a date or not?

"I wanted you to know what happened because I was going to ask you…" I stumble over the words.

"Ask me what?"

Sweat breaks out on my forehead and chest. I pull at my shirt, suddenly aware of how it's sticking to me and showing off my least favorite asset—my stomach.

"Ask if you want to grab a bite sometime," I say. "Like after school. We could do the Donut Prince together. Put a dent in some double chocolate glazed—"

"About that," she says, and she pauses, suddenly aware of students around us in the hallway.

She motions for me to follow, and to my surprise she takes me to the quiet corner under the stairwell where students like to make out between classes. I've never been here with a girl. I always just pass by quickly, trying to ignore the sounds of other people having fun.

Now I'm about to have fun. I panic, cursing myself for not carrying mints like Ishaan.

"You know my situation," Daisy says, her voice barely above a whisper. "I'm new and I can't afford—how do I put this in a nice way? I can't get a bad rap."

My hope fades as I realize we're not here for kissing. I'm not even sure Daisy knows this is the school hookup spot.

"What are we talking about?" I ask.

"I can't afford to get a bad rap because I had one in my last school."

"How'd that happen?"

"I made some mistakes, one thing led to another, and I was suddenly someone I didn't want to be. You know how things can get out of control. In school. Online. Someone repeats a lie enough, it starts to sound like the truth."

"Like with me and Harry."

She nods. "It got so bad in Philly we had to move. I mean, we didn't have to, but my mom said if I got in trouble again, she was shipping me out to one of those wilderness programs."

I think of Daisy, far away, sleeping in a tent. Not cool unless I'm in the tent with her.

"We definitely don't want that," I say.

"Thanks," she says, like we just settled something, even though I don't know what it is.

"So what's next for us?" I ask. "Donut Prince after school?"

"I don't think so," she says. "You got drama around you."

"But I'm a playwright!"

"Not that kind of drama. The other kind. Anyway I'm not into dating right now. I have to focus on school."

"Sure, I get it," I say, trying to hide the fact my whole life is crashing down around me. What happened to her calling me Donut Prince and laughing at all my jokes?

"Is this because I tackled Harry?" I say, my voice sounding a little desperate.

She frowns. "It's got nothing to do with that. It's about me. If you don't get that, then you don't understand me at all."

"I'm trying to understand—"

She shakes her head, shutting me down.

"I'll see you around, okay?" she says, but it sounds like the opposite.

If I had more time, maybe I could think of a killer line to win her back, but all I can do is repeat what she said.

"See you around," I say.

Those are my last words to Daisy Luna before she walks out of my life.

I stand there, not believing what just happened. My life rewrite totally bombed.

A voice interrupts. "Dude."

I look up to find two senior guys with their arms around each other. The taller guy gestures to the space under the stairs.

"Are you using it?" he asks.

"Not even close," I say.

He starts to turn away, then looks back. "You're that kid from the gym class," he says, his eyes widening.

"Yeah."

"Gutsy move. Can't wait to hear about it."

"Hear about what?"

"Life in the witness protection program," he says with a grin, and they disappear under the stairs.

CHAPTER TEN:

YOU GOTTA KISS THE CAST

By midafternoon things have gotten so bad in school, Ishaan and Mia call an emergency meeting at the wall.

"What's the latest?" I ask them.

"I've heard two rumors," Mia says. "The first is Harry's dead, you killed him, and you're going to prison for the rest of your life."

"I'm pretty sure that one's not true," I say.

"Second, he's got a broken arm, he's declared war, and you've got a target on your back."

I think about the incident in the bathroom earlier in the day. "It's the second one," I say.

"Hang on now," Ishaan says. "I believe we're overreacting. I heard that the arm wasn't broken. Technically, it's a wrist fracture. And Eugene, although impressive to us, is like a gas bubble to these guys."

"Do you think you're helping?" Mia asks him.

Three football jocks pass by, glaring at me. One of them is Dillon. He subtly cracks his knuckles. Sounds like he's warming up for a fight.

Mia stands defiantly, hands on her hips, glaring at them and protecting me. The football players move on, at least for now, avoiding a public run-in.

"That guy totally has it in for me," I whisper.

"He's the one who bullied you freshman year," Mia says angrily.

"Looks like he mounted a junior year revival."

"The whole school is talking about it," Ishaan says, earning him a frown from Mia. "What? It's the truth."

I laugh nervously. "They say there's no such thing as bad press, right?" But I sink down against the wall until I'm sitting on the sidewalk.

"Daisy thinks I'm a drama king now. She doesn't want anything to do with me."

Mia rolls her eyes. "You're in big trouble, and you're worried about what some new girl thinks?"

"She's not just some new girl," I say.

"Then what is she?" Mia challenges me.

I sigh, looking away. "Forget it."

"It's rare for me, but I agree with Mia," Ishaan says. "You're in trouble, dude. This isn't high school drama anymore. It's more like a suspense thriller, and you're the one being hunted by a football death squad."

"I hear you both," I say. "But what do I do?"

"We need to hire bodyguards," Ishaan suggests. "Three or four large individuals to follow you around like the Secret Service."

"For the next two years?" I ask.

"Good point," Ishaan says. "Hey, Astoria is nice. Maybe you can live with your dad?"

"Not an option," I say.

My phone buzzes. It's a text message from an anonymous number: *Watch your back. You won't see us coming.* My hands shake as I show Ishaan and Mia.

Mia bites at her lower lip, all attention focused on me.

"Here's the deal," Mia says. "You need to apologize to Harry."

"Terrible idea," I start to say.

"Today," Mia says firmly. "Stop this before it goes any further."

"But they're jocks," I say. "They already suck up all the energy in the room. Why do they need my apology on top of it?"

"You took out one of their own," Mia says.

The thought of apologizing makes my stomach churn. I look toward Ishaan, hoping for a better answer, but he nods solemnly.

"Mia's right. You have to kiss the cast."

I chew my lip as I think about what they're suggesting.

Apologize or escalate.

Apologize, and maybe this dies down, replaced by the next high school scandal to come along.

Or hold my ground, restate my innocence, and maybe this escalates into a war I can't win and may not survive.

Mia and Ishaan look at me, waiting for my decision.

"Mia's right," I say. "Guess I'm off to football practice to talk to Harry."

I have no idea what Harry—or the rest of the team—will do when I show up. I think about standing in front of the entire team, trying to apologize in front of jocks who I don't know and who already hate me. I shudder as I think of the comments that might come my way.

On the other hand, they might not wait for an apology and seriously mess me up. If I have to choose between shame and the emergency room, I should probably choose shame.

"You want us to come with?" Mia asks.

It's tempting—but I don't want to subject my friends to what might happen.

"I have to do this one alone," I say.

I swallow hard, rising from the pavement and heading back toward the school.

CHAPTER ELEVEN:
TOO BIG TO FAIL

I walk up the staircase to the rooftop field. I've never been up here after school, but I guess there's a first time for everything.

I emerge onto the roof and take in the sight of the Upper West football squad, more than three dozen players in uniform interacting with a half dozen coaches barking orders. My knees are literally shaking. I thought that only happened in the movies. I try to swallow, but my mouth has gone dry.

The magnitude of chaos on the roof is astounding. Whistles blow. A group of players charges at large padded blocks, throwing themselves into exercise like they've got a score to settle. Others are running drills along the side of the field, sweat pouring down their faces as they push themselves to their limits. A few more are doing pass plays, sprinting downfield, eyes fixed on a ball that's never thrown. The dedication is obvious, but it's hard to understand the allure.

Then I see Harry beside Coach.

He's injured for real. Unlike his fellow players, Harry's wearing street clothes, his arm encased in a bright orange cast that he holds by his side. He's watching practice from the sidelines, shouting occasional advice when a player passes by, but otherwise sitting with a sullen expression on his face.

One by one the players stop what they're doing, their gazes turning toward me with a mixture of anger and confusion. I glance over and see Dillon scowling at me. My heart pounds as I slowly approach Harry.

"Hey, um—"

I try to call to him, but my throat is dry and it comes out in a croak.

I take a deep breath and head across the field. By the time I arrive, Harry, Coach, and the entire team is staring at me. It's like the play *Twelve Angry Men*, only I'm living a version called *Thirty-Six Angry Football Bros*.

"You're banned from this field," Coach says.

"I get it," I say. "I just need to talk to Harry for a second—"

Coach steps up, his face contorted with anger. "Did you come to finish the job, Guterman? Maybe you could break the other arm so he has a matching set."

I swallow hard, struggling to get the words out.

"I came to say I'm sorry," I tell Coach.

"You should register your stomach as a deadly weapon," Dillon says from somewhere behind me, accompanied by snickering.

I wince when I hear the laughter. I'm back on the playground in third grade, kids laughing as I get stuck on the slide.

"Yo, Coach," Harry interrupts.

Harry stands, his shadow blotting out the sky. I look up at him towering over me.

"Talk," he says. "I'll listen."

I swallow hard. "I'm Eugene," I say.

"So?"

"Like I was telling Coach," I say, my voice breaking. "I came to apologize."

Harry lifts his orange cast. For a second I think he's going to bash me over the head with it, but instead he holds it out in front of my face.

"See what you did to me?" he asks.

The cast is covered with get-well messages, girls' names with phone numbers, and hearts.

"It looks like I turned your arm into a dating app."

He squints in anger. "I don't need a broken arm to get dates."

"So it's broken?" I ask, horrified.

"Stable fracture of the wrist," Harry says. "Not quite as bad, but not good."

"So what happens now?"

"Now I break your wrist as payback."

I gasp. The apology isn't working. I start to panic.

Harry smirks, the first crack in his angry facade. "Nah, I'm not gonna beat you up in public. I'll wait until later and do it when you least expect it."

"Really?" I ask fearfully.

He shakes his head like I'm an idiot. "So what's up? It took guts for a guy like you to come to practice. Or maybe you've got a death wish."

"I love life," I say, my voice shaking. "And donuts. And writing plays."

"I don't need a college application. Say what you have to say."

"I'm sorry." I lower my head. "Really sorry."

"Why'd you do it?"

"I was showing off. Trying to."

"Trying to tackle me from behind like an a-hole?"

"You were an unintended victim. I just wanted to...to prove something to myself, I guess."

"Prove what?"

"That I could run. And be a part of regular gym."

"What other kind of gym is there?"

"Coach is doing this new adaptive gym project. We're supposed to separate from the regular class and improve our skills."

Harry looks at me for a long moment. "You're not exactly the athletic type. Maybe it would help you."

"I know. I just wanted to feel normal."

"So that's it. I figured you were working for Stuyvesant High or something."

"Your rivals?"

"No crap," Harry says.

"You thought I was a Sumo assassin?"

He laughs. "It's competitive out there."

"So what's the prognosis with the arm?"

"Fracture like this," he says, holding it up. "They don't want me playing for eight weeks."

"Eight weeks? That's not so bad."

"It's a lifetime," he says angrily, and my fear ratches up all over again.

"I'm playing anyway," he snarls. "Non-dominant hand. I don't give a crap. I'll throw with my feet if I have to. They're not sidelining me."

Harry's intensity is impressive. I got intimidated from being offered a theater club show and caught a case of writer's block. Harry broke his wrist and he's practically chewing through the cast to stay in the game.

"I really messed things up," I say. "I wish there was some way—"

Before I can finish the sentence, the wind is knocked out of me, and

I stumble forward, almost bumping into Harry again. Luckily, he jumps out of the way.

I shout in surprise and turn around fast.

Langford is on the ground, rubbing his shoulder. Did he just run into me?

Before I can figure out exactly what happened, I'm hit again from the other side. I stumble, but I'm more surprised than hurt. I look back and see Dillon on the ground this time, scowling up at me.

Langford jumps back up and tries to tackle me. I shout in fear, but I sidestep on instinct and bump him with my hip, sort of like pushing through a subway turnstile.

"Hold up," Harry shouts at them. "What are you guys doing?"

"Payback," Dillon says, rubbing his side where he crashed into me.

"I didn't ask you—"

"You don't gotta ask us," Langford says. "We got your back, Double H."

I freeze, unsure what to do. I got Harry wide-eyed on one side, two football players on the ground in front of me, and the exit stairs far away on the other side of the field. Everything in my body is screaming for me to run, but how am I going to outrun people who practice running twenty hours a week?

Coach hustles over. "Did you see that?!" he asks breathlessly. "He took them down like it was nothing."

Harry looks at his fellow teammates on the ground, and his mouth drops open as if he's just realized something important.

"Guterman is too big to fail," he says.

"Are you thinking what I'm thinking?" Coach asks him.

Harry grins as the two of them trade conspiratorial looks. I have no idea what's going on right now.

Coach comes toward me. "You came here to apologize, right?"

"For sure," I say.

Coach licks his lips. "I have an idea how you can make it up to Harry and the team. Come with me."

"Where are we going?"

He points across the field to some big pieces of equipment.

Harry leans toward me, a grin spreading across his face. "This is about to get interesting."

CHAPTER TWELVE:

AN UNEXPECTED OFFER

Before I realize what's happening, Coach has taken me over to the shed, handed me a football uniform and pads, and suggested I put them on. Next thing I know, I'm standing on the field dressed like an Upper West varsity football player.

I feel like I'm at a sports-themed Halloween party, but Harry and Coach look on approvingly.

"How does it feel?" Coach asks.

The pads on my shoulders feel heavy, the helmet on my head is like a second skin designed to block my hearing and create perspiration, and the shin guards feel like someone has put tourniquets on my legs.

"Feels great," I say unenthusiastically.

"Takes a little getting used to," Harry says.

I don't plan to be wearing this stuff long enough to get used to it, but Coach asked me to try it on, and he and Harry seemed to imply this was part two of a two-part apology.

"Okay, so I'm dressed like a football player. Are we gonna do embarrassing photos, or what exactly?"

Coach and Harry are still smiling at each other, and it's making me uneasy.

"No photos," Coach says. "You see that thing downfield?"

I follow his gaze to what appears to be a cross between a jungle gym and a human being, fused together in some kind of unholy alliance from a graphic novel.

"We call it a tackle dummy or a sled."

"What does it have to do with me?" I ask.

"You're going to run into it," Coach says.

"Like you ran into me," Harry adds.

I look at the tackle dummy, which is basically a large blue pad about the size of a human being, and I wonder how hard or soft it really is. I guess I'm about to find out.

Coach gives me some quick instructions, most of which I don't understand. Something about letting the shoulder pad contact the dummy, and staying low, and chopping feet and driving through. I feel like I need Google Translate to know what he's talking about, but there's no time to pull out my phone.

"Get ready," Coach says.

I blow out a breath, ready as I'll ever be.

"Set—" Coach says.

I crouch down for my third run this week. The previous two have been disasters, but the third time's the charm, right?

"You can do this," Harry says calmly.

"Go!" Coach shouts, and toots the whistle.

I run at the dummy, expecting it to feel like a big soft marshmallow, but that's far from the truth. It feels more like concrete. I hit it hard and bounce off, the wind instantly knocked out of me as I fall flat onto my butt.

The good news? The football equipment I'm wearing helps. Kind of. It doesn't hurt as much as it would have if I wasn't wearing it.

The bad news? It hurts a lot.

As for the big blue pad on the dummy? There's nothing soft about it.

"So much for that little experiment," Dillon says, shaking his head.

I look up from the ground, slightly stunned, shame creeping in at the demonstration of my lack of athleticism. The uniform suddenly feels tight around my stomach and I pull at it, hyperaware of my pudgy stomach spilling out the sides.

The football players have stopped working out, and they're watching me from the sideline. Oh well. Nothing goes together quite like failure and an audience.

Coach helps me to my feet, and I rub my chest.

"That thing doesn't move at all," I say. "So I get it. That was my payback, right? Like a practical joke to teach me a lesson?"

"It doesn't move on its own," Harry says. "You have to move it."

I look back at the tackle dummy. There's *no way* that thing moves.

"I just ran into it, Harry. I tried to make it move." I turn to Coach. "We're done here, right?"

"I'd like you to try again," Coach says as if it's my choice.

I've got football players glaring at me, and Harry standing there with the orange cast heavy by his side.

"One more time," Harry says quietly.

"Whatever," I say with a sigh. "I guess I'll cross it off my bucket list."

"The kid's funny," Harry says. "I like him."

I confront the horror of the tackle dummy once again. I don't need to draw this thing out the second time. I take a few steps back, hoping to get a little extra runway, and I go for it.

I aim lower this time and launch myself at the dummy, my pad impacting it midway up. I really put my back into it, trying with all my strength to push the sled.

The stupid sled does not budge.

The only thing different this time is that I don't fall on my butt. I stay on my feet and I take my punishment like a guy who deserves it, and who is maybe a little less afraid than he was the first time.

I step back from the dummy, hands out at my sides.

"I came, I saw, I was conquered," I say. "Feel free to quote me on that."

Harry has an amused look on his face as I walk up to him. "You quitting?"

"I know when I've failed," I say. "Can you help me get this stuff off?"

"Sure," he says with a shrug. "I give you props for being willing to try."

Harry sounds sincere, and I almost like him for a second. Then I remember where I am—and who I am—and I snap out of it.

I reach for my helmet, and Coach interrupts.

"Hold up just a second," Coach says.

I look at him warily.

"Last time," Coach says, pointing downfield at the tackle sled.

"You said I only had to do it twice and I'd be done."

Harry nods. "You did say twice, Coach."

Hang on. Is Harry really taking my side?

"I know what I said. But I'd like— What's your first name again? I forget."

He doesn't even know my name?

"Eugene," I say.

"Eugene, I'd really like you to try it again for me."

"It's an immovable object, Coach. How's it going to be any different the third time?"

"I've got a different idea this time," he says.

I look to Harry, who shrugs. "Up to you," he says.

Okay, now I'm in hell. This experience is worse than the production of *Jersey Boys* I saw in Hoboken.

I've just about had it with this entire day, but I shrug my shoulders.

"Let's get it over with. You want me to hit it high, low, in between, chop my feet, drive through, whatever those words mean?"

"None of that," Coach says. "I want to ask you a serious question."

Harry leans in, curious.

"Big picture," Coach says. "How's life going for Eugene?"

I let out a humorless laugh, thinking of a lifetime of being over-weight, culminating in the last week—breaking Harry's wrist, becoming an enemy of the people, and Daisy wanting nothing to do with me. My chance for love gone. My life totally messed up.

And why?

Because I'm fat.

"Well?" Coach asks.

"I hate my life," I say.

My own words hit me hard. It's a huge statement, truthful enough that I'm near tears once I've said it out loud.

"There's something you can do about it," Coach says.

"I can?" I ask.

71

Coach points to the sled across the field. "You see that blue tackle pad in front of you? That pad is whatever's bothering you. I want you to run at your problems and show them who's boss."

I think back to all the times I've run away from my problems in the past. Or gone to Donut Prince.

Running *toward* my problems seems like a really bad idea.

But then I look downfield, and the tackle dummy suddenly becomes a giant donut that I want to destroy once and for all. A growl rises from inside me, and I take off, running at the tackle dummy with all my might.

This time when I hit the thing, I don't bounce off.

I ram into it with an explosive slap, and I lean in and push off, roaring in anger and frustration, driving with my feet under me, pushing back at the anger bottled up inside me.

At first nothing happens, and then, to my surprise, the dummy moves—just a little, but enough for me to know that it can move. It's not stuck, it's not permanent, and best of all, it's not more powerful than me.

I hear the whistle blow, and I step back in awe, looking down to make sure I haven't imagined it.

The dummy is off-center, pushed back a couple inches on one side.

It really happened.

I turn around to find Coach and Harry grinning widely.

"You're done for the day," Coach says.

"You killed it out there," Harry says.

"Is this how sports work? You nearly die, then people congratulate you?"

"Pretty much," Harry says.

Harry and Coach start stripping off my football pads. It's a relief to feel the air on my skin again.

"Have you ever played a sport?" Coach asks.

"I did Improv Olympics one summer," I say.

"A real sport. No talking."

I shake my head. "Not my thing."

"How do you know if you've never tried?" Coach asks.

"I've tried phys ed," I say. "And I know I hate that."

Coach frowns like I hurt his feelings.

"I'm a theater club guy," I say, trying to soften the blow. "Theater's my thing."

Harry and Coach trade looks. I'm not sure what's going on, but I start to feel uncomfortable.

"So—we're done here?" I ask, eager to get off the field and away from the strange afternoon.

"I'll walk you out," Harry says.

He leads me toward the stairs, but he pauses for a minute, standing on the edge of the rooftop. The sun is setting and the city buzzes with activity below us.

Harry stares out over the city, and he begins to speak without looking at me.

"The team relies on me," he says. "I'm the quarterback and the captain. You probably know enough to know how important that is."

"Maybe you're putting too much pressure on yourself," I say, surprised at the sincerity in my voice. "One player doesn't make or break a team, right? It's a collective effort."

"You said you're a theater guy. What if the lead actor breaks his leg and can't go on—"

"We have understudies—but I see what you mean."

"Some players matter more than others, and I'm one of those players. Maybe it's not fair, but that's just how it is."

The sun dips below the horizon, casting long shadows that stretch across the field.

Coach catches up to us as we head toward the locker room stairs.

"So, Guterman," Coach says. "You pushed that sled today. You think you could push an opponent?"

"Like a human one?"

"Exactly."

The question catches me off guard. "Me? You saw what happened out there."

"I saw a guy face the tackle dummy head-on and not give up. That says something about you."

"And you're funny," Harry says. "That doesn't suck."

"Wait—what are we talking about?" I ask.

"We're talking about you joining the team," Harry says.

"The football team?"

"I'm not saying you're the next Tom Brady or anything. But I need a good offensive lineman."

"What's that?"

"Offensive linemen protect the quarterback," Coach explains. "You'd be protecting the guy whose wrist you fractured."

"Yours truly," Harry says, holding up his bright orange cast. As if I've forgotten why I'm here.

I can't believe what I'm hearing. It's like I just auditioned for a role and I didn't even know I was at an audition. It's flattering and all, but there's no way I'm saying yes to football.

"You got a whole team," I say. "Why do you need me?"

Coach signals to Harry.

"Like I told you, the doc says I shouldn't play, but that's not an option," Harry says. "I can't afford to get tackled and reinjure the wrist. So I need a wall in front of me."

"I'd be your wall," I say, suddenly getting it. "Harry, I don't know how to play football. I've never even *watched* a football game."

"That's what practice is for," Coach says. "We'll teach you everything you need to know."

I shake my head. "Sorry. I'm not a sports guy."

Harry shrugs. "If you played ball, you wouldn't have to do that adaptive gym thing you were telling me about."

"No?"

A grin sneaks across my face. Being upstairs in phys ed, that means closer to the sky. Closer to Daisy and a second chance.

"Question you should be asking yourself," Harry says, "do you wanna do the adaptive thing, or you wanna stay upstairs with the big dogs?"

Coach nods. "What about it, Guterman? You ready to transform your life?"

The jocks have surrounded us now, standing silently by. That's about four tons of peer pressure in a confined space. My theater career flashes before my eyes. I haven't had much of a career yet, so it's a quick flash.

Then I think of Daisy. Her laugh, the way she looked in her leather jacket the first day I saw her—

"I'm all about the big dogs," I say. "I'll do it."

The players explode in an excited roar, and Harry beams.

"No way!" he says. "That's great."

Coach extends a hand. "Welcome to the team, Guterman."

I smile so hard my cheeks hurt. The players are clapping and patting my back as they head for the locker room. I'm suddenly in one of those moments you see in a sports movie. The awkward underdog getting his chance to be something else.

"You just gotta get the all-clear from the doctor, then we'll get you into practice," Coach says.

"A doctor?" I ask, suddenly concerned.

"It's a physical," Harry says. "No biggie."

"It's called a pre-participation physical evaluation," Coach says. "It's a form from your doc saying you're safe to play. You've got a doctor, right?"

"I've got a doctor who specializes in egg white frittatas," I say, a plan already forming in my head.

Coach gives me a curious look. "You're a weird guy," he says, "but I'm glad to have you on board."

He squeezes my shoulder, then strides away. The football players are gone now. But Harry hangs back, Dillon standing by his side, almost like a bodyguard.

"Give us a second, Dill," Harry says.

Dillon grunts as he goes by, looking at me like he doesn't trust me. I can't really blame him.

Harry and I are alone on the field now, the glow of the setting sun casting an aura around him.

"I knew you had it in you," he says.

"That makes one of us."

"We gotta work on that confidence," he says with a laugh, then vanishes down the stairs.

Mia said we had to peak this year. I just didn't think it would happen the first week of school.

CHAPTER THIRTEEN:

I TRICK MOM

"Mom, I need to go to the doctor," I say, attempting to sound casual. She looks up from a plate of vegetables and tofu, her mouth framed with concern.

"Are you sick?" she asks with an edge in her voice.

"Not exactly. But I need a doctor."

"Did you know that I'm a doctor?" She gestures to the scrubs that hang off her like a second skin.

"I guess I'd forgotten," I say.

She laughs, and I pick up a forkful of tofu, feigning delight at the dinner she's prepared.

"It's not like I'm sick," I tell her carefully. "I need a physical for gym class."

"I thought you hated gym?"

"Maybe you haven't been keeping up on my socials, but I'm a lover of gym class now."

"As much as I enjoy reading your posts, I've been busy bringing children into the world."

"Most parents are obsessed with what their kids are doing online."

"I trust you," Mom says, which is not what I want to hear when I'm in the middle of lying. I almost ditch out on the plan until I think of Daisy.

"I want to get some exercise," I tell Mom.

"That's a positive thing."

"And there's this girl—"

Mom's face lights up like a Broadway marquee, and I instantly regret saying anything.

"A girl? Tell me everything," Mom says.

I groan. "C'mon, Mom."

"Is she Jewish? Is she nice?"

"For sure. Her father's a rabbi. Third generation."

"Are you making fun of me?"

"Definitely. So here's the deal. I like a girl in class. I don't know her very well, but she's athletic, and it's inspiring me to try some new stuff. And no, she's not Jewish."

"But she's athletic? I can work with that."

"Coach asked me to get a sports physical. It's kind of a rule now if you're going to do new things. Paperwork and all."

"If it's just a formality, maybe I could sign the form for you? You just had a physical a couple months ago."

I conveniently pull the form out of my pocket and pass Mom a pen. She puts on her glasses and scrutinizes the form. I hold my breath.

"I don't see anything here that I object to," she says, but then she hesitates, pen hovering above the form, and she glances down at my stomach.

Not the stomach glance.

It's a prime feature of my life. Strangers, teachers, my peers, and even my parents. All of them glance at my stomach like they can't believe how big it really is. Not just once. Over and over like it's a new surprise.

Mom clears her throat. Here it comes.

"Honey, how strenuous is this class? I'm a little concerned about your wei—"

"My remarkable good looks?" I say, interrupting her. "It's a burden on all of us, Mom. I blame you because beauty is inherited."

She laughs and looks back at the form. "It's nothing too difficult, is it?"

Competitive varsity football? Definitely not.

"It's moderate, healthy exercise," I lie. "Supervised by a fitness professional who was a former member of the Australian polo team."

"That coach with the accent who gave you a bad grade?"

"That guy. But now he wants to help me."

"Got it," she says. "Well, good luck. With the class and with the girl. I want to hear everything."

"For sure," I say.

As if I'm going to tell my mom anything about Daisy ever again.

Mom passes me the form, and I breathe a sigh of relief.

I slip the signed paper into my backpack so I can transport it to school tomorrow. Now I just have to figure out how to tell my friends what happened—then survive football practice. No problem at all.

CHAPTER FOURTEEN:
DAISY MEETS THE NEW ME

I'm standing on the field before gym class, my heart pounding when I spot Daisy across the field warming up with a group of girls. A few days ago I couldn't wait for phys ed and the chance to see her again. Now I know she doesn't want anything to do with me, and seeing her just feels painful.

Ishaan is late as usual, which means I'm up here feeling alone and exposed, sweating in the sun. I catch a glimpse of bright orange—Harry's cast as he comes onto the field with Langford and Dillon and a few of the football bros. I think back to what happened at football practice yesterday, but it seems far away, almost like a dream.

Suddenly Harry notices me, and he waves me over. Maybe it wasn't a dream after all.

I hesitantly walk toward the football players, unsure of what they want from me.

"What are you doing hanging all by yourself?" Harry asks.

"It's my discomfort zone," I say with a half laugh.

"No more. You're with us now."

The players make way, opening up a little space for me to stand next to Harry.

"This is different," I say, unsure of how to handle the new positive energy.

I glance across the field from this new perspective. It's not me alone, or me and Ishaan clinging to each other in a sea of uncertainty. I'm in a huddle of jocks, strong, powerful, and respected. That's when I notice kids are looking our way. Not just kids.

Daisy, too.

Coach comes toward us, smiling wide.

"You were outstanding yesterday," Coach says. "A real surprise."

"I had to ice my entire body last night."

"Been there, done that," Harry says with a smirk.

"Did you take care of the form?" Coach asks.

"All set." My cheeks feel hot as I think about lying to Mom last night.

"Great, then we'll see you at practice after school," Coach says.

"Today?"

"No better time than the present."

"For sure," I lie. "Can't wait."

Harry's smiling, the football bros are welcoming, Coach is acting nice—

It's like my whole reality flip-flopped overnight.

The whistle blows, and I walk onto the field, buzzing with this new, unfamiliar energy, but no longer exiled to the weight room for adaptive gym.

"What was that all about?" Daisy asks.

I turn, surprised. I guess Daisy is talking to me again.

"No big deal. I had to work out some stuff with my bros on the football team," I say casually.

She looks surprised. "Your bros?"

"We're friends," I say. "Friends and teammates."

"Huh?"

"I'm playing varsity football this year."

"What? You said jocks and theater people didn't get along."

"What can I say? I'm bridging the gap. Football, theater—I'm a triple threat."

"What's the third threat?"

I hesitate, realizing this could make or break my chances with Daisy. I think about the way Harry walked onto the field the first day, brimming with confidence.

"If you get to know me better, maybe you'll find out," I say with a cocky smirk.

"The Donut Prince has got some swagger." I can feel the electricity between us, like when I first met her.

"I guess I'll see you around," she says with a smile.

"Definitely," I say.

She saunters off, and I turn to find Ishaan staring at me, a combination of shock and confusion on his face.

"What the hell is going on?" he says. "Daisy is into you again? And did I see you talking to the football jerks?"

I should tell Ishaan what happened at football practice yesterday, but the story is so complicated and now isn't the time or place. Besides, shouldn't I find out if I'm going to stay on the team before I drop that kind of news on him?

"The football guys?" I say. "We're sort of friends now. The apology worked better than I thought."

"So you got them off your case," Ishaan says.

"For sure."

"And adaptive gym?"

"Canceled. I'm staying upstairs."

"I'm impressed," Ishaan says. "You pulled your life together in under twenty-four hours."

"Not my whole life. I've still got a play to write," I say.

"I'm talking to Wabash next period," Ishaan starts to say, but he's interrupted by Coach's whistle.

I promise myself I'll tell Ishaan about football as soon as I know what's up with the team, but for now, I end up lying to him through the entire gym class, watching his strange looks when the football bros help me out or throw a thumbs-up my way.

All except Dillon, that is. He eyes me like I'm a shoplifter in a Duane Reade drugstore, tensing every time I get within a few feet of Harry Habib.

CHAPTER FIFTEEN:
COME TO CLUB

I'm heading up to the locker room after school, butterflies in my stomach.

Mia and Ishaan rush down the hall, falling in on either side of me.

"Aren't you coming to theater club?" Mia asks.

"I thought it was the end of the week," I say, panicking because I'm due at football practice.

"Wabash moved it up," Mia says. "He's really trying to get a drop on the theater department this year."

"I can't," I say. "I've got stuff."

"What stuff?" Ishaan asks.

I look from Ishaan to Mia, their faces curious.

I'm stuck. "Nothing that can't wait," I say.

"Great!" Mia says, pulling me along.

"I talked to Wabash about the play," Ishaan says. "He's a little worried at the moment, but you can finesse the situation. Just apologize like you did with Harry Habib yesterday."

"Apologize?" Mia says. "You did it already?"

"It worked and he's off the hook," Ishaan tells her.

"Good for you!" Mia says.

I groan inwardly, feeling bad that I haven't told my friends what's going on.

Now I'm stuck going to club with them when I have to be up on the field in just a few minutes. I run the scenario in my head, deciding I'll go to theater club for a quick minute, make an excuse for an early exit, then race up to the field so I won't be late for practice. I'll be cutting it close, but I think I can make it work.

The truth is, it feels good to be going to the black box theater with Mia and Ishaan by my side. I've walked this path hundreds of times over the last two years, and my body remembers it like a Stanislavski sense memory exercise. It's familiar while everything else in my life is unfamiliar right now.

So I fall in next to them, hitting the double doors and stepping into the theater like I belong there.

Only I don't. One look from Wabash makes that very clear.

Today Wabash is adorned in a top hat and a cape like the Phantom of the Opera. He's holding court at the front of the theater, a dozen actors and half as many techies assembled in a circle around him. Leave it to Wabash. Even his meetings are staged in the round for maximum impact.

He turns when he sees me, his face contorting into a theatrical scowl.

I take a deep breath. "What's up?"

"With that banal line, our production of *Waiting for Guterman* concludes," Wabash says.

"Sorry I'm late," I say.

"It's not you who's late. It's your play."

I back up a step, and Mia grabs my arm, preventing me from running off.

"Ishaan said you wanted to stop by and beg my forgiveness," Wabash says loudly.

Geez. How many people can I apologize to in a week?

I glance at Ishaan, who feigns innocence.

"That's why I'm here," I say.

"Excellent," Wabash says. "Stick around. We'll talk in a minute."

The sights and smells of our black box theater give me a case of the feels. I went to the theater a couple times over the summer, but being in the audience is much different than putting on a show. And this black box feels like home.

I recognize most of these actors from previous shows, but there are a few newbies who may be freshmen. I see Danny Mercurio, the only real male lead in our school (and who starred in my last show), Melinda Del Rio, who usually plays the funny mom characters, and Shanice Johnson, who has the best singing voice and isn't afraid to use it in echoey hallways, in bathroom stalls, and at every cast party since sixth grade.

"For those who are new," Wabash says, "allow me to introduce *the* Eugene Guterman—playwright, raconteur, and defender of the downtrodden."

The actors break into enthusiastic applause. They're looking at me with excited smiles on their faces. It's pretty shocking considering that I've been dramatis personae non grata in these parts for nine months.

"What did I do to deserve this?" I ask once the applause dies down.

"You spoke truth to power," Wabash says.

"And then you broke its arm," Danny says, which brings nervous laughs around the room.

They obviously don't know about me joining the football team, but how would they know? I haven't even told my best friends yet.

Danny Mercurio stands up. "First they took our funding, then they started using the theater for pep rallies, then they converted our green room into a locker room—"

"Where does it end?" Shanice shouts.

"One of them called me a theater geek," Danny says.

"You *are* a theater geek," Melinda says with pride.

"But only we get to call ourselves that," Shanice says, as heads nod around the room.

Wabash gives me an approving glance. "You stood up to Harry and his henchmen...You found the courage to do what we couldn't."

I get it now. They think I broke Harry's wrist on purpose like everybody else. As much as I enjoy being welcomed back as a conquering hero, I can't let the lie continue.

"The thing with Harry—it wasn't intentional. I wasn't trying to knock him down."

"Of course you weren't," Wabash says with an exaggerated wink that sends laughs around the room.

I groan. This story is obviously a big deal to all of them. I glance at my phone. How would they feel if they knew I had to ditch them and get to football practice right now?

"Looks like I interrupted season planning," I say. "I'll let you get back to it."

"No need," Wabash says. "The season plan is all you."

He drapes his arm across my shoulders, effectively drawing me away from the others. "I know you came to apologize for being late with your script, but I think I owe you an apology."

"For what?"

"I put too much pressure on you."

"It's not your fault," I say. "I'm just having a little trouble feeling like I'm good enough."

"The one-act last year?"

"It was more like a five-act."

"You're a rule breaker, Guterman. And an arm breaker."

"I don't think so."

"The lady doth protest too much," he says. "Let me be up-front with you. The Upper West theater department has lost its way. *Seussical*?"

I shiver when I think of last year's spring musical extravaganza.

"You hated it, too," Wabash says. "And the year before that, an all-brunette production of *Legally Blonde*? They struck a powerful blow against the patriarchy, didn't they? It's performative, but it's not performance."

Wabash's passion on the topic is inspiring. I remember how proud I felt when he asked me to write a play at the end of last year. Then pride met reality.

"We need fresh ideas, Guterman. I want the drama club to be an edgy alternative. That's where your play comes in. Let's show them what theater can be when we put real passion into it. And let's get the focus off the jocks and back onto the arts."

The more he talks, the more excited I get, but why is it happening now, ten minutes before my first varsity football practice?

I look back at the expectant stares of the drama club members. Ishaan is glowing with pride. Mia urges me on with her eyes.

"You think I can do it?" I ask quietly.

"I believe in you, m'lad. I just need you to believe in yourself."

I nod hesitantly. "I'll try."

"Before you run off, give me the logline for your play."

I take a deep breath. Should I tell Wabash about *Jacked Jill*? Or maybe my Chekhovian adaptation of *Mad Max* called *Irritated Ivan*?

No, I'm going to stick with Manny's advice.

"I was maybe going in a more personal direction this time," I say.

"Personal in what way?"

"A classic love story. Boy meets girl kind of thing."

"It's a little binary if you don't mind my saying."

"It's *Romeo and Juliet* plus donuts. So it's tertiary."

"Interesting. Could there be a gender nonconforming character?"

"There already is. A certain brilliant theater director who inspires the protagonist."

Wabash glows. "I like where this is going. Tell me about the protagonist—"

"He's an overweight playwright who falls in love with a new girl at his school, but he loses his way and starts to question where he belongs."

"I see it now. A contemporary twist on a classic love story that upends body image and gender tropes."

"That sounds a lot smarter than what I'm writing, but I'm inspired."

Wabash grins proudly. "Every writer needs a dramaturge," he says.

I push through the double doors into the hall. I quickly glance at my phone. Football practice started five minutes ago. I'm about to leave when Wabash pops his head out the door.

"This play—could you have it ready in a month?" he asks.

"Why?"

"Rehearsals start the first week in October," Wabash says. "Is that a problem?"

"I...can...do that," I say.

Wabash bows and, with a grateful flourish, he retreats into the theater.

The moment the doors close, I take off running toward football practice. I make it halfway down the hallway before I get a bad case of the shakes.

What did I just agree to?

I had twelve weeks to write a play over the summer and I wrote exactly zero words. How am I going to write an entire play in a month? And be on the varsity football team at the same time?

CHAPTER SIXTEEN:
A CRASH COURSE IN FOOTBALL

I steady myself and step onto the football field, feeling completely out of my element. Everywhere I look, players are running drills and practicing moves. I don't know the bro code or the rules of the game, and despite being wider than a lot of these players, I'm not sure if I can take a hit like I did the other day. Not when the stakes are real.

Coach blows his whistle and waves me over. I notice the players watching as I walk across the field.

"Glad you made it," Coach says.

"Here's my form," I say, passing him the paper Mom signed for me. "I can guarantee my ovaries are healthy."

"Huh?"

"Inside joke," I mutter.

"Great, so where to start," he says, rubbing his hands together. "Football involves a lot of running, Guterman, and it seems like running is a bit of a problem for you."

"I'm pretty good with running," I say. "It's stopping that's the problem."

A couple nearby players laugh. Score one for Guterman. If I can make three dozen jocks laugh, maybe I'll survive this experience long enough to write a play again.

"Tighten it up," Coach barks, and the players go silent.

All except for Langford. "We're just having a little fun, Coach," he says.

"You know what's fun for me?" Coach says. "You. Taking a lap."

He blows his whistle, and without a word, Langford sprints to the edge of the field and starts running in a wide circle.

My guts tighten. Wabash Simpson is snarky as hell, but he never forced anyone to take a lap.

"Let's get into some drills," Coach says. "D team downfield, O team up, do what you know how to do. Guterman and Double H with me."

I'm not quite sure what he said, but I know I'm supposed to follow Harry, so that's what I do.

The players divide and run off to start their warm-up, and Harry and I stand facing Coach.

Coach says, "We've gotta teach you the basics, Guterman. Harry, you're out of commission for the physical stuff, so you're going to be my assistant coach today."

"Great plan!" Harry barks.

First rule of football: never speak when you can shout.

Across the field, a group of players runs in place at full speed, then drops to the ground with a grunt, then jumps up and runs again. It looks miserable, but I don't hear any of them complaining.

Coach blows a sharp tap on his whistle. "Dillon! I need you."

Dillon does a slow jog toward us. He's approximately the size of a mountain in his football pads. I think about running into him in the bathroom the other day, and I'm afraid all over again.

He grunts. "How can I help, Coach?"

"Our friend needs a crash course," Coach says.

Dillon cracks his neck. "I specialize in crash."

"Guterman, I leave you in good hands," Coach says, and he jogs downfield to yell at some players.

I turn back, and Dillon gives me a once-over. The last time he did that was freshman year, and it ended with my head in a toilet. But Harry is looking on from the side, so I figure I'm safe for the moment.

"You're like a smart guy, right?" Dillon asks. "APs and all."

I'm surprised Dillon knows anything about me other than my weight problem.

"I'm pretty good at school," I admit.

"But Harry says you know jack about football."

"Never paid attention to it."

Dillon shakes his head like he's amazed. "You gotta treat this like school and memorize everything I say. I talk fast, and it's all going to be new to you."

"Bring it on," I say. This is the kind of challenge I can work with.

"Offensive tackle," Dillon says. "It starts with your stance."

"My stance?"

Dillon drops into a squat position. "Leg position. If you're not centered and balanced, you can't explode off the line."

Dillon pantomimes a football play as he describes the lineman's job. "Everything you do is timed to the snap," he says. "That's the moment the center presses the ball into Harry's hands. If you move before that, it's a penalty. If you move after, you're out of luck. So get into your stance, listen for the snap, and you're in motion the moment the ball is in motion."

"How do I know when that is?" I ask.

"This kid's a total newb," Dillon says, frustrated.

"Let me translate," Harry says, stepping in. "When you do theater, you have to wait for the curtain to open or some light to go on—"

"Waiting for your cue," I say, shocked that Harry knows anything about theater.

"Football's the same. You can't move until you hear your cue. You get into your stance—"

"That's what we call 'places,'" I say.

"—and the snap is your cue," Harry says.

"Finally, you're talking my language," I say with a smile.

Dillon has regained his composure. He squats in front of me, a serious expression on his face.

"Your feet have to be in the right position," he says. "So you can Get Off fast."

"I can what?"

"Linebacker slang," Dillon says. "Your first step. We call it the Get Off."

"You gotta learn how to Get Off," Harry says.

He and Dillon bump fists.

"Are you guys messing with me?" I ask.

"Nah," Dillon says. "First step is the Get Off. Second step is the Strike. Then you get your hands involved and it's called the Stick. Then your final step is called the Finish. People have different names for the moves, but they're basically the same every time. Four moves—bam, bam, bam, bam."

"Like dance choreography," I say.

"Yup," Dillon says. "Only in this dance, your partner is trying to kill you."

My eyes widen.

"The linemen on the other team are trying to get past you to get to me," Harry says. "Your job is to stop them."

I rub my head, already overwhelmed from the lesson and I haven't done anything yet. I thought football players were dumb guys who threw their bodies at each other. But the way Dillon and Harry are describing a play, it sounds a lot more complicated.

"It might take me a minute to get up to speed," I say.

"More than a minute," Dillon says. "I'm gonna teach you the basics today, and you're going to practice it over and over again. Same four moves that make up a block, until you're blocking in your sleep."

That doesn't sound fun to me, but it's not like I can leave.

"You think you're ready to try this thing for real?" Harry asks.

Honest answer? No. The answer I give Harry?

"More than ready!" I shout, and Harry smiles.

I was right; this shouting thing works in sports.

Dillon calls over a player to challenge me. Not just any player.

Langford.

We line up and Langford spreads out across from me. I'm a big guy, but Langford is big—and tall—and powerful.

"Gotta be honest with you, Guterman," he says quietly. "Dillon and I had a talk. We don't think you belong here. And I'm about to prove it to everyone."

"Wait, I thought you were supposed to be helping me."

"I'm gonna help you get to urgent care."

I swallow hard, but my mouth has gone dry. Coach and the rest of the players are watching us. I look back, and Langford's scowling face is inches from mine.

I settle into the stance like Dillon showed me, bracing my legs and keeping my arms down until I'm ready for the Strike. Harry calls the play from the sideline, and when he yells hike, Langford launches himself at me from across the line.

It's like the tackle dummy from the other day, only it's angry and it's running at me. The first time I'm hit, my teeth chatter in my jaw, and a vibration passes from the top of my head to my toes. Next thing I know, I'm on my back looking up at the sky.

I struggle to all fours, trying to get my breath back. Harry comes over to check on me.

"That frigging hurt," I whisper.

Harry nods. "Damn right it hurts. Just about every time, but you can't show it. You suck it up and you never let the other guy see you struggling."

"Why not?"

"Because it's a mental game as much as a physical one. And if your opponent smells weakness— Know what I mean?"

"Sort of," I say, and I walk to the line to try again.

"Back for seconds?" Langford says. "I guess you've been practicing at the buffet."

"Shut up, dude."

Harry calls the next play, and before I realize what happened, I'm on my butt again, looking up at Langford.

"Make me shut up." He smirks.

It's a mental game as much as a physical one.

I suddenly get it. Langford is playing me—physically and mentally—and he's winning.

Maybe he's right that I don't belong here, but right now I don't feel like quitting.

I feel like running into something.

At the next whistle, I get pushed back again, but this time I don't fall. If Langford is impressed, he doesn't show it.

On the play after that, I'm standing and pushing back. Unsuccessfully, but pushing.

By the sixth whistle, Langford and I crash into each other, and neither of us moves forward or back. It's a stalemate.

Coach double taps the whistle to stop the drill.

I'm exhausted, heaving for air, but I didn't move. I didn't let myself get pushed around.

Langford grabs my helmet and shakes it in his hands.

"Good hustle!" he shouts. "I figured you had it in you!"

"Wait—I thought you hated me."

"Hate you? I'm trying to train you up, bro."

I look over at Harry and Coach smiling like I did a good job. Even Dillon gives me a grudging nod.

"I guess pudge don't budge," Dillon says.

I stare him in the eye. "What did you say?"

"Pudge don't budge," he replies. "And you're Pudge."

"*Pudge.* That's a good one," Langford says.

"Really? You too?" I say.

So I was right before. He does hate me. They all do.

"What's wrong?" Langford asks.

"I don't like that name," I say. "I'm not into bullying."

"What bullying?" Dillon says. "It was a compliment!"

"Everyone gets a nickname," Langford says, but I'm not trying to hear that. I've had enough name-calling and whispers behind my back over the years. After nearly killing myself in practice, I expected better.

"I'm out of here," I say, heading for the stairwell.

"Hold up," Harry says.

But I don't hold up. I crash through the door and take the steps two at a time as I head down to the locker room. My head's spinning with all this stupid sports stuff.

I'm racing through the hall when I stop suddenly. Ishaan and Mia are standing by the locker room door, arms folded tightly in front of them. They scrutinize me, surprised and horrified at the same time. I'm dressed in a full football uniform with pads and a helmet. Sweat breaks out under my arms and my collar suddenly feels too tight. I've been caught in my lie in the middle of the school hallway.

"*Friday Night Lights: The Musical*?" Mia asks snidely.

I shake my head.

"That's why you left club so quickly," Ishaan says, astonished. "You crossed over to the dark side."

My stomach rumbles with an unpleasant combination of hunger and nausea.

"It's kind of a long story," I start to say.

"Lucky we have plenty of time," Mia says, her voice scolding. "We'll wait for you in front of the school."

I swallow hard, dreading what's about to happen.

CHAPTER SEVENTEEN:
SLEEPING WITH THE ENEMY

Ten minutes later I step outside to find Mia and Ishaan standing on the sidewalk. Their posture stiffens when they see me.

I thought football practice was hard, but facing the two of them is like cliff diving.

"I'm sorry I didn't tell you," I say.

I figure it never hurts to start with an apology. I'm getting a lot of practice this week.

"I can't even look at you," Ishaan says.

"You are looking at me."

"Metaphorically."

"You're sleeping with the enemy," Mia says.

"It just happened," I say.

"Diarrhea just happens," Ishaan says. "Joining the football team and turning your back on everything you care about in the world? That does not just happen."

"I didn't turn my back on anything!" I protest.

"Those people hate us," Ishaan says.

"I think it's more like we hate them."

"So it's mutual," Mia says. "Fact is, they have not been kind to the plebes, and now you're one of them?"

"I was following your advice," I remind her. "I apologized to Harry, and one thing led to another."

"You said the apology calmed things down," Mia says.

"It did. And it came with an offer."

"So he instantly accepted your apology and asked you to join the stupid football team?" Mia asks.

I think back to the apology followed by running at tackle dummies until I couldn't see straight and my body was one large black-and-blue mark.

"It didn't go that smoothly," I say.

A couple football players come out of school, nodding when they see me.

"Good hustle out there," one says, and I give him a thumbs-up.

"Really?" Ishaan says. "This is like a *Black Mirror* episode."

Mia pulls me around the corner to my not-so-secret wall next to the bodega. She glares at me with Ishaan backing her up.

"Are you doing it for that girl?" she asks.

"Partially," I say, my voice low. "And they made me an offer I couldn't refuse. I don't have to go to adaptive gym if I protect Harry while his wrist heals."

"I get that," Ishaan says, like he's coming around to my side of things.

"No way. Sounds shady to me," Mia says.

"Maybe I want to try football," I say.

"You are going to hate it," Mia says. "Total waste of time."

"You're the one who said it was our year to peak," I counter. "Now I'm peaking, Mia, and you don't like it."

Mia clenches her fists, furious. "Don't throw my words back in my face," she says. "You betrayed our trust, and now you're making excuses."

Betrayed?

"This is getting a little intense," I say, trying to defuse the situation.

"Seriously," Ishaan says. "He messed up. Let's not stick him in the prop closet for the rest of his life."

Mia takes a deep breath and her expression softens. "Those people don't care about you like we do," she says. "I'm afraid you're going to get hurt. And not just by football."

I wince as I think about Dillon calling me "Pudge" up on the field.

"Plus what about drama club?" Ishaan asks. "Wabash pulled you outside to talk to you. He hasn't walked out in the middle of club since that time Billy Porter was in the building."

"What did he say?" Mia asks.

"He gave me more time for the play—and I agreed to write it."

Mia slaps her forehead. "Are you a theater person or a football person?"

"Maybe I'm an everything person."

"You're going to hate everything about football," Mia says.

I don't exactly love it, but I don't want to admit that to her. Not yet.

Ishaan steps between us, attempting to quell the rising tension.

"We're the Three Musketeers, remember?" he begs.

"One musketeer stopped walking the other musketeer to school," Mia says.

"I've been busy," I say.

"Whatever. You've got your own agenda. Enjoy it."

She walks away without saying goodbye. It's maybe the first time that's ever happened since I met her.

I take a deep breath and look at Ishaan. "Harsh."

"She got her feelings hurt," Ishaan says. "You have to admit, it's weird to join the football team and not tell your friends."

I sigh and sit down with my back against the wall.

"I don't really know what I'm doing, Ishaan."

"I get it. I mean, Daisy Luna—that's the kind of girl you join a club for. Even a club you hate."

"I don't hate football," I say. "It's more complicated than that."

"How is it complicated?"

I quickly fill Ishaan in on what happened in practice, including the guys calling me Pudge at the end. I don't expect him to act like a best friend after I lied to him, but he does exactly that, listening carefully, scratching at a barely present beard as he takes it all in.

"So what did you do after Dillon said the Pudge thing?" Ishaan asks.

"I kind of lost it. I stormed off. I ran into you and Mia right after."

"Running away isn't a good idea."

"No kidding. These guys can smell weakness. In my case, they could also see it in 3D."

I wince and shift positions. My body is aching all over, a painful reminder of my foolish decision.

Ishaan looks on, concerned. "But you stood up to that Langford guy in practice, right?"

"Yeah, but what good did it do me? Now everyone on the team is calling me Pudge. It feels like bullying all over again."

"It might be bullying," Ishaan says. "But could it be branding? Guys like that give you a nickname, then you're in."

"Even if it's true, then what? I'm 'Pudge Don't Budge' for the rest of my life? I prefer Eugene Guterman, Pulitzer Prize–winning playwright. With Daisy Luna as my muse."

"Maybe Mia had a point. How are you gonna write a play when you're in football practice all the time?"

"I'll write on the weekends."

"Isn't that when they do their games?"

I sigh. "Maybe I'm not cut out for football. But how do I get out of it?"

"It's easy. Just tell Harry you gave it your best shot, but you're not into it."

"These jocks are not really the quitting type. They're more like run till blood comes out of your eyeballs type."

"Dude. Let's get you back to the theater world where you belong."

More football guys pass by, laughing hard and talking sports stats in loud voices. I've got nothing in common with these guys. It couldn't be more obvious.

"You're right," I tell Ishaan. "I should focus on theater. I just gotta find a way to break it to Harry without getting destroyed."

CHAPTER EIGHTEEN:

HARRY IS A GOOD TALKER

I walk into the cafeteria the next day and see Harry holding court at the football table across the way. Now is as good a time as any.

I sneak a quick look at Ishaan and Mia, who are camped out in our usual spot in the corner, keeping a watchful eye on me, and I head for the jock table.

"Pudge!" Harry says, brightening when he sees me.

I wince when I hear the nickname. "Hey, can we talk privately?" I ask.

"Step into my office," he says with a shrug as he guides me toward the cafeteria exit.

I feel the collective curiosity of the school on us as we pass. Harry is like a magnet for attention. The closer you stand to the magnet, the more you attract.

By the time we get outside, I'm losing my nerve, so I start to talk fast.

"Here's the deal. This might not be my thing."

Harry raises an eyebrow. "This? Football?"

I swallow hard, my heart pounding. "Yeah. The Pudge thing doesn't work for me."

"It's just a nickname."

"It's a nickname that means fat."

Harry dismisses me with a wave. "We all got nicknames. I'm Double H. Dillon is the Big D. Langford is Nimbus 'cause he's like a storm cloud—dark and dangerous."

"But their nicknames aren't insulting and mine is."

"Bro, what do you need? You want me to make up a different nickname?"

"It's not just the name, Harry. It's the whole sports thing."

Harry steps back. "You're not sure if you want to keep playing football," he says.

I swallow, my heart pounding in my ears.

"Yeah."

He sighs, but he gives me an understanding nod.

"No problem," he says. "It's not for everyone."

He shrugs and starts back toward the cafeteria.

What?

"Hang on," I say, chasing after him. "Let me explain."

"If you want," he says, not breaking his stride.

"Football practice was a wild experience," I say. "But at the end of the day, I'm a theater person."

"You told me that the first day you came to the roof."

"Well, it's true," I say, owning it.

"Got it. Well, let's grab some lunch."

He continues toward the cafeteria.

"I can still sit with you?"

"Of course, Eugene. We're friends now, right?"

"Maybe," I say, increasingly baffled at how this interaction is turning out.

Harry reaches for the cafeteria door, then pauses.

"There's just one other thing," he says, his tone suddenly serious. "Football's not just a hobby for me. It's my life, my mission. And this is my last year to prove what I can do."

I suddenly get what Harry is saying. "It's your last year to peak."

"I know you didn't do it on purpose," he says, holding up his bright orange cast. "But you still did it, Guterman. Now I need a solid from you."

"A solid?"

"I need my wall. You get it?"

"I think so."

"It's bigger than nicknames, bigger than your feelings."

The most popular guy in school is asking for a favor, straight out.

"How long till you're back at full strength?" I ask.

He shrugs. "Six weeks, eight. Doctor can't say exactly."

"Eight weeks is a lot of wall."

"Can you just give football a chance?" he asks. "If you hate the Pudge thing, we'll delete it. But the guys like the name. And they like you. 'Pudge Don't Budge' could be our rallying cry this season, take us all the way to States."

I consider his request, and what it would mean to agree to it. "You really want me on the team, don't you?"

Harry nods confidently. "You're a natural. Train up, learn how to take a hit, and keep going. And we'll work on your swagger. Teach you how to walk into a room like you own the place."

"So you're offering life lessons, too?"

"One-stop shopping," Harry says with a grin. "Football and life. But mostly football. What do you think?"

Suddenly Daisy Luna turns the corner. She's wearing a long skirt and high-tops that make her look sophisticated and cool at the same time. She seems surprised to see Harry and me together, but then her face lights up and she gives me a shy wave as she passes by.

I watch her go, maybe a second too long.

"Oh, I get it," Harry says with a smirk. "You're into that girl from gym class."

"A little," I admit.

He closes his eyes, pondering for a second, before they snap open. "How about this? I'm having a party at my place Saturday night. Players and friends. It's an Upper West football tradition. And you, Pudge, are personally invited."

I wince at the nickname, but it hits a little different attached to a party invite.

"Yeah, maybe I can come," I say.

He points down the hall to where Daisy is turning a corner. "You should also bring a plus-one."

I smile as I think about bringing Daisy to a popular high school party.

"You get it, right?" Harry asks.

"I'm starting to."

Harry winks and opens the cafeteria door.

"I think we can help each other this semester, Guterman. Just wait and see."

CHAPTER NINETEEN:
MAYBE DAISY

Harry guides me over to the jock lunch table, where they part to make way for me. I've never had football bros clear a bench for me. I wish I could say it didn't matter, but it feels good, like I suddenly belong.

I look helplessly toward Mia and Ishaan, who are watching with a combination of horror and astonishment. Harry makes a little announcement about our deal at the table, and the football bros burst into a round of applause, drawing the attention of the entire cafeteria.

A second later my phone starts buzzing in my pocket, messages coming in at a rapid clip. I look across the room where Ishaan is hunched over his phone, finger moving at light speed.

Awkward.

I turn to Harry. "Maybe I should go and find that girl—"

He smiles. "Do that."

I speed-walk across the cafeteria, pausing briefly in front of Ishaan and Mia. Ishaan scowls at me.

"I think my allergy medicine is giving me hallucinations," Ishaan says. "Because it looked like you were hanging with the jocks again."

"I swear I'll be right back," I say. Mia's mouth drops open like she's staring at a stranger. I dash out of the cafeteria and out the front door of the school, eager to catch up with Daisy.

I'm vaguely aware I'm acting out of control, reversing my decision and ditching my friends, but there's so much happening so quickly, I just go with it.

I find Daisy three blocks away emerging from Broadway Farm with a plastic bowl of fruit cradled under her arm.

"Is that Daisy Luna?" I say, trying to hide the fact I'm totally out of breath.

"Hey," she says. Not exactly enthusiastic, but it's a distinct improvement from our conversation under the stairs where she gave me the "see you around" speech.

"I saw you earlier," I say.

"I saw you, too. With Harry. So the football thing is true, huh?"

"You thought I was making it up?"

"Not exactly. I just didn't think of you as—"

"The rugged athletic type? Looks can be deceiving," I say, trying to sound confident.

What did Harry call it? *Swagger.*

"Triple Threat Eugene," Daisy says with a grin. "Your life is really interesting."

"What about yours?" I say.

"Not so interesting."

"What do you mean? New school, new city. How's it going?"

A sad smile tugs at her lips. "I don't feel like I fit in."

"Maybe you'd fit in more if you hung around with me," I say.

Her eyes widen. "Wow, you've changed. So tell me, what's this hanging around with you look like?"

"For starters it looks like you coming to a big football party on Saturday."

Her smile fades. Not the reaction I was hoping for.

"Gotta be honest. I'm not really a party kind of person anymore," she says.

"Anymore?"

"I used to be all about it. But things got a little out of hand."

I try to appear casual even though I'm totally curious. "You seem so buckled down with school and everything."

"Like you said, looks can be deceiving. I mean, I was always buckled, then I'd have a drink. Or two. Then I'd unbuckle."

The image makes me blush a little.

"So what? You're reformed now?" I ask.

"Something like that," she says. "It doesn't mean I can't have fun. As long as it's not liquid fun. What's the party look like?"

"Solid fun," I say, and she laughs. "If we go together, it'll be amazing. I can introduce you to some people, too."

"You're very convincing," she says. I can tell she's starting to feel more comfortable with the idea.

"So it's a plan?"

"What the heck," she says. "Sounds like fun."

I do my best not to whoop with joy. We exchange details, and I say goodbye, knowing for the first time I'm going to see her outside of school.

I'm elated, at least until I walk back into school and realize I have to face Mia and Ishaan.

CHAPTER TWENTY:
THE LONG GAME

I rush back to the cafeteria, anxious to talk to Mia and Ishaan before things get out of hand.

Too late.

When I sit down, they barely register my presence. I clear my throat a couple times, but they pretend I'm invisible.

"Is he back?" Ishaan asks Mia.

She nods glumly. "This time it's not your allergy medicine."

"So…lots to talk about," I say.

"We had a whole conversation, but I saw you deep in enemy territory," Ishaan says, pointing over his shoulder to the table of football bros. "Was I talking to myself?"

"Would you let me get a word out?" I say.

Mia interrupts. "Ishaan said you guys made a decision without me."

"We made a *big* decision," Ishaan says. "And Eugene made a bigger decision without either of us."

"Harry gave me a different perspective," I admit. "So there's a little bit of a twist."

"I can't wait," Ishaan says.

I take a breath, steadying my voice.

"I'm quitting the team like we talked about," I reiterate. "Just not yet."

"Explain," Ishaan says.

"Harry needs me."

Mia looks incredulous. "We need you," she says. "The theater club needs you."

"You were barely talking to me after practice last night."

"I got angry, and I got over it," Mia says. "Like friends do. But you didn't even text me this morning, so I called Tamar to walk to school with me."

"Who's Tamar?"

"A STEM friend," she says casually.

I used to know everything about Mia's life, but now she's doing things with people I don't even know.

I sigh and put my head in my hands. "I'm sorry, Mia. I'm really sorry, Ishaan."

"Do you believe him?" Ishaan asks Mia.

"I was hoping for tears," she says. "But yes, it sounds like a legit apology to me."

"Thank you," I say. "Now that we're back in business, can I tell you the good news? We're going to a party on Saturday."

Silence.

"Hello?" I ask.

"Which we?" Ishaan says.

"We *three*."

"Like an opening night party?" Mia asks.

"Not a theater party. A school party."

"Which school?" Ishaan asks.

"Our school."

"We have parties?" Mia asks.

I put my forehead on the table. My friends are much more out of it than I realized.

"Okay, you two, here's the deal. Harry is throwing a party, and I thought we should represent."

"Represent what?" Mia asks.

"The essential role of thespians in our school social hierarchy," I say half-jokingly.

"Hang on," Ishaan says. "You're saying Harry Habib invited us to a party."

"Yes, he did," I say confidently, even though he only invited me and a plus-one.

Mia frowns. "Nice try. He barely knows our names. Plus, we're not the kind of people they invite to football parties."

"Speak for yourself," Ishaan says.

"I'm invited, so you're invited," I say, feeling unexpectedly good. "It's our chance to mix it up with a different crowd. Think of it as a sociology experiment—with free pizza."

I glance at Mia to see if she's buying it. She looks slightly more curious than she did a moment ago.

"I'm all about mixing," Ishaan says. "Football players means girls, and girls means—"

"Objectification," Mia interrupts.

"Jazmin?" Ishaan mouths silently across the table. His hand drifts to his pocket, where he takes out his ever-present pack of mints.

I nod, even though I'm not sure if Jazmin will be there.

"I don't know," Mia says.

"I want to share my new life with my friends," I say. It doesn't seem to be convincing Mia, so I try a different tact. "Honestly, I'm a little scared to go alone."

Mia perks up.

I feel bad manipulating her like that, but it's also true. I'm super nervous to go to the party and deal with the jocks alone.

"C'mon, Mia," Ishaan begs. "Our boy needs backup."

We both stare at her, pleading.

"Okay, fine," she says.

Ishaan pumps his fist and I breathe a sigh of relief.

"This is going to be so much fun," I say. "I'll coordinate and get back to you both."

"Hang on," Ishaan says. "What is there to coordinate?"

"Times and stuff."

"Times? We'll meet up and go together."

"It's not just us," I say.

Mia's expression sours. "Who else is going?" she asks.

"Daisy Luna," I say quietly.

"Dude!" Ishaan frowns. "You know I'm on team Daisy, but I'm not about chaperoning your date."

"I think it's a great idea," Mia says.

"Wait, what?" I ask.

"I never did my background research 'cause I thought you two were over, so this will give me a chance to ask her some questions."

"It's a party, not an interrogation," I warn Mia.

"It's a social gathering, and I intend to be social. And curious," Mia says with a smile.

Ishaan, Mia, and I have gone to plenty of cast parties together, so it'll probably be fine, I tell myself. I mean, how different could a football party be?

CHAPTER TWENTY-ONE:
DRESS FOR SUCCESS

I stand in front of a giant pile of clothes on my bedroom floor, most of which have been on my body in the last twenty minutes, and none of which fit me right.

In my mind, I imagine characters getting ready for parties in plays and movies. It's always a transformation scene. Ugly duckling to swan. Geek to prince. Nerd to hipster. But for some reason, everything I put on just makes me look like me—only worse.

I groan and flop down on the bed, depression and frustration growing with every second.

I reach for the phone and shoot a text to Ishaan.

What should I wear? I ask him.

How do I know? he texts back.

What are you wearing?

Concert attire.

I sigh. Never ask a violinist what to wear to a football party.

You should ask Mia, he texts back.

Can't, I say.

Even after the cafeteria apology, Mia and I are awkward with each other, and we're still not walking to school together.

Ah, well. Desperate times call for desperate measures.

"Mom!" I shout.

Whatever you do, don't ask your mom, Ishaan texts me.

Later, I say.

Mom cracks open the door. She looks at me, then at the pile of discarded clothes on the floor.

"Oh, honey," she says, her voice filled with compassion.

"It's hard enough to talk to you about this. If you pity me, I swear I'll lose it."

"All right then." Mom straightens up and steps into the room. "No pity. Tell me what's going on."

I take a breath, reluctant to tell her the truth. She waits patiently.

"I'm too fat to go to a party," I say, my voice wavering.

"No such thing," she says.

"Well, nothing fits."

Mom looks down at the clothing pile. "What have you tried?"

"Everything I own. The next step is to stitch together two bed sheets and call it a toga. Unfortunately, it's not a costume party."

Mom peers into my mostly empty closet.

"Why don't you wear what you wear to school?"

"Then I'll look like I do all the time."

"Like a handsome young man—"

"I warned you, Mom."

"Got it." She makes a zipping motion across her lips. "The world hasn't changed that much since I was your age. I think you should wear something simple and comfortable like a sweater and jeans."

"I already tried the sweater. It fits like an eighteenth-century corset."

"Show me."

I groan at the thought of trying on clothes in front of my mother. I thought I grew out of this like six years ago. How did the best night of my life suddenly turn into the worst night of my life?

I reluctantly pull on the sweater, holding my arms out to the side like an overstuffed scarecrow.

"I see," Mom says. "It's a little tight. Did you do the knee trick?"

"What's the knee trick?"

Mom gestures for me to sit down on the side of the bed, then she pantomimes pulling the bottom of the sweater over my lap and across my knees.

"Like this?" I ask, following her lead.

"Now spread your legs slowly and stretch the fabric."

"This is weird, Mom."

"Trust me. I'm a doctor."

"Really? I had no idea."

I do as Mom suggests, awkwardly pulling my legs apart like I'm on a weight training machine. I feel the fabric giving way beneath me.

"Now stand up," Mom says.

When I get up, the sweater fits over my stomach. There's even room to spare.

"Cross your arms tight," Mom says.

She tugs at the shoulders, stretching out the back of the sweater. Then I reverse my arms and she pulls at the front, adjusting the fabric across my chest and even enlarging the collar to make room for me. A few more tugs and tweaks, then she steps back.

"There we go," she says. "Much better."

I look at myself in the mirror. I'm not exactly in Harry Habib territory, but at least the sweater fits and I look decent.

"How did you know how to do all that?" I ask.

"Women deal with these things," Mom says. "And I was teenager once, too."

"I thought you came out of the womb wearing scrubs."

"Funny man." Mom grins and heads for the door. "Enjoy your party. And how about next week we go out and get you some new clothes?"

"I don't think so," I say.

Mom waves over her shoulder and a second later she's gone.

But I don't have time to dwell. I have a party to get to.

CHAPTER TWENTY-TWO:
THE PARTY TO END ALL PARTIES

We meet on the street outside Harry Habib's building on Central Park West. I'm standing with Mia and Ishaan when Daisy walks up wearing a long black dress with red high-tops and a leather jacket. Ishaan shuffles uncomfortably, pulling at the black concert pants and white button-down beneath his trench coat. We stand there awkwardly.

"Um, you look great," I say. "Everyone know everyone?"

"Just by reputation," Daisy says. "You must be the amazing Mia."

Mia smiles faintly, but I can see she's skeptical.

"And I recognize you from phys ed. Ishaan, right?"

"Ishaan Iyengar at your service," he says with a deep bow. "Available for classical recitals as well as engineering issues, should any unexpectedly arise."

I clear my throat, but Ishaan doesn't get the hint and stays in his bow.

"Okay, then. Let's mingle," I say, anxious to maneuver us inside before this gets even more embarrassing.

An expensive lobby and a staffed elevator ride later, we step through the doors of Harry Habib's lavish apartment overlooking Central Park. It's not like I live in a bad location, but this place is next level. The scene is unreal, like every Netflix series about beautiful kids with money. I look across a living room filled with the crème de la crème of Upper West High—popular girls, rowdy football bros, supporters, and friends—all of them dressed like they've got something to prove.

Ishaan's eyes widen in awe. "Is this heaven?"

Mia shakes her head. "It's just a party, Ishaan. Don't drool on the carpet."

"Do you mind if I have fun, Mia? Unlike you, I'd like to enjoy my adolescence."

"Don't fight, guys. You'll embarrass us," I say, and I glance nervously at Daisy.

"Do you party like this all the time?" she asks.

She seems wowed by the same things we are. She just hides it better.

"More or less," I say, which earns me an incredulous look from Mia. "I mean, it's my first time at Harry's house, but he told me they do this every week at a different person's place, so it's going to be a busy fall."

"Parties every week," Ishaan says. "It's like another dimension parallel to our own."

"Yeah, a more superficial dimension," Mia says, eyeing a ferocious arm-wrestling match in the middle of the dining room table.

I remember Daisy's uncertainty about committing to a party, so I step a little closer to her.

"How's it going?" I ask her.

"I'm good," she replies, a hint of nervousness creeping into her voice.

Before we can take another step, a group of kids stumbles past, shouting and holding up beers.

Mia looks like she's ready to head for the door.

"Some of these kids have parents in tech," I tell Mia. "There are a lot of tech accelerators in the city."

"You know that for sure?" Mia says, perking up.

"Definitely," I say, even though I don't know. I mean, statistically, some of them have to be in tech.

"So try to mingle," I urge her.

"I'll try," she says, looking around cautiously.

"PUDGE!"

Harry strides toward us with a wide smile on his face.

"What did he call you?" Daisy whispers.

"It's my nickname," I say, slightly embarrassed.

"You made it," Harry says, embracing me in a bear hug.

"I brought my posse," I say. "This is Ishaan, violinist and engineer *par excellence*. This is Mia, a tech genius and my best friend. And this is—"

"The track and field star," Harry says. "I remember her gasping for breath and running behind me."

"Maybe I let you win because I didn't want to embarrass you in front of the whole class," she says.

"Maybe that's what happened," Harry says with a laugh. "How about I give all of you a tour of the place."

"Hell yeah, I want a tour," I say.

"Sounds good," Daisy says.

"I'll sit this one out," Mia says.

Ishaan looks disappointed, but he falls in next to Mia.

"I'm signed up for the VIP walk-through in a half hour," he says.

"All good," Harry says. "It's a parent-free zone tonight—they're in the Bahamas. That means alcohol on the table over there; pizza, sushi, and hot wings in the kitchen; and please do your vaping on the balcony."

"I prefer to vape in the open air," Ishaan says. "It's more refreshing that way."

I shake my head. It's painful to see Ishaan trying so hard.

Harry gestures like an impresario and motions for us to follow him. The music gets louder as we pass through the larger room where people are dancing. There are a lot of curious looks and side glances from the crowd.

I pull at my clothes, suddenly uncomfortable. It feels like my sweater shrunk down a size since I walked in.

"You okay?" Daisy whispers.

"I'm used to camouflaging my body, not bringing it out into the open at parties."

She looks at me curiously, but it's too loud to explain, and I'm not sure she'd get it even if I did.

Harry leads us into a private den where a wall of windows overlooks Central Park. The park is spread out below us, the lights of the east-side buildings glowing in the distance.

"Incredible view," Daisy says.

"I guess," Harry says. "The problem with beautiful stuff—if you see it every day, you stop appreciating it."

"Are you talking about the park or your girlfriend?" I ask.

"Good one, Pudge," Harry says, and he gives me a mock punch in the arm. "But my girlfriends are still beautiful."

"Was that girlfriends—plural?" Daisy asks with a raised eyebrow.

"Hey, it's 2024. The old rules don't apply."

"Ick," Daisy says.

"New rules," I say, trying to lighten the mood. "Who knew?"

"This guy's so funny," Harry says. "Did he tell you how he's helping me out?"

"Not really," Daisy asks.

"Yeah, he's my new go-to guy. I'm glad you two are hanging out."

I glance at Daisy but it's hard to read her reaction. On one hand, Harry is the most popular guy at our school. On the other—ick.

"Enjoy the scenery if you want," Harry says. "I'm gonna go back to the party."

He gives me a little wink and goes out the door, leaving us alone.

I take a deep breath, alone with Daisy for the first time.

"We don't have views like this in Philly," she says. "At least not that I've seen."

Daisy smiles playfully. "So you finally got me alone, Donut Prince. What are you going to do with me?"

My mouth goes dry, and I'm suddenly at a loss for words. Daisy leans toward me—

The door flies open, and three kids come crashing in. "Hey, mind if we party in here?"

They don't wait for a response, pulling up seats and crowding around a coffee table.

"Awkward," Daisy says.

I look from them to Daisy. Maybe I should tell these guys to leave, but I don't feel like I'm in a position to get away with it.

"I guess I should make sure Ishaan and Mia are okay," I say.

"Whatever," Daisy says.

We walk out together, and I silently curse myself. How did I get the perfect handoff from Harry Habib, then drop the ball before I'd even run a yard?

Once we make it back to the main room, I catch a glimpse of Mia and Ishaan across the way, standing near a wall as stiff as bowling pins. Now I feel bad for leaving them in the first place.

Daisy and I are walking back to them when she stops abruptly by the drinks table.

"I have an idea," she says, and she reaches for a beer bottle.

"Wait, I thought you said—"

"It's not for me. It's for you."

"I don't really drink," I say.

"Why doesn't that surprise me? Can I tell you a secret, Eugene?"

She gestures for me to come closer, and I shiver as I lean in and smell her perfume.

"I think you should have a drink," she says in my ear. "Because it will relax you."

"I like being tense. It burns fat."

"It's a Corona Light. Low cal," she says with a mischievous grin. She cracks open a seltzer for herself. "Up to you, of course. I'm not here to push booze on anyone."

I laugh even though that's kind of exactly what she's doing. I look from Daisy to the bottle of beer on the table. I haven't had a drink since I downed a shot of kosher wine at my aunt's shabbat dinner two years ago.

Anyway, here I am now. At a football party. Next to the hottest girl I've ever met and who actually came with me.

Are we on a date? I'm not even sure.

"I think a beer is just what the doctor ordered," I announce as I reach for it. Daisy intervenes to pop a lime into the neck of the bottle, and I take a swig.

"How's it taste?" she asks.

It's ice cold, bitter, and mostly unpleasant.

"Not my favorite," I admit. "Do people actually like this stuff?"

"It takes some getting used to. Try another sip."

This time the combination of bitterness and citrus is more familiar. Not exactly delicious, but not as bad.

"Okay," I say. "I think I'm starting to get the idea."

A third swig, and the flavor spreads into my cheeks and face, and I realize I'm pleasantly lightheaded. Daisy is watching me with amusement.

"What's up?" she asks.

"I'm drinking my first beer," I say. "That's what's up, Donut Princess."

"Dude, you get buzzed fast."

"Maybe?"

She laughs. "You're cute at a party."

"You're cute everywhere."

"Pace yourself with the beer."

"Totally," I say, but I'm used to eating and drinking everything fast. I'm drinking the beer like it's diet soda, and I'm nearly finished with the bottle. When Daisy turns around, I grab a second and follow her.

I'm a little lighter on my feet now, and I'm not quite as self-conscious as I was a few minutes ago. For the first time in my life, I'm getting a sense of why people drink.

I catch up to Daisy, and she points across the room.

"What's your friend up to?" Daisy asks.

She's pointing to Ishaan. I suddenly realize I forgot all about Mia and Ishaan and left them alone.

I look over now and I see Ishaan, all his attention focused across the room. I follow his gaze to see who he's looking at. It's Jazmin Cole, his cheerleader crush. I'm torn between admiration and terror as I watch Ishaan reach into his pocket and slip a mint into his mouth.

"She's here!" I say. "That's Ishaan's crush."

"The girl with the cornrows?" Daisy asks. "This is going to get weird."

"I can't watch."

"You have to!"

Ishaan takes a deep breath, doubles up on the mints, then crosses the room with purpose, heading for Jazmin.

"He doesn't lack for ambition," Daisy says. "You think she'll talk to him?"

"He can be very persuasive."

"I think it's gonna go badly."

"I bet it won't."

"We'll see," she says with a grin. "You might owe me some money at the end of the night."

I take a slug of beer, and I feel vaguely guilty. I'm standing on the sidelines betting on my best friend's life when I should be his wingman.

"I need to help him," I say.

But what can I do? I'm pretty much a stranger here, and it's not like I know Jazmin.

I look around frantically, hoping I'll see Harry and can solicit his help, but he's nowhere nearby.

Anyway, it's too late. Ishaan is already behind Jazmin. He combs his fingers through his hair, then whips his head back and forth a couple times until his bangs fall into place.

"He's doing the hair thing," Daisy says. "Totally hysterical."

She grabs my hand and pulls me closer so we can hear.

I gasp as I try not to overreact to the sensations racing up my arm from the sudden contact with Daisy's warm hand. Did I just become a guy who holds a girl's hand at a party?

I take another sip of liquid courage, and I lean into her.

"Here he goes," Daisy whispers.

She leans into me and her breasts push up against my arm. I take another slug of beer.

"First violin," Ishaan is saying, practically shouting to be heard over the music.

It takes Jazmin a second to realize he's trying to talk to her, then she looks at him, uncertain.

"What's up?" she asks.

"First violin," he repeats. "It's my favorite position."

"Ick. What are you even talking about?"

Daisy puts her chin on my shoulder.

"I'm first violin in the orchestra," Ishaan announces. "Not to brag, but that makes me the best string player."

"So?"

Ishaan looks panicked. His best line just got shot down.

"Are you into music?" he asks.

"Everyone's into music."

Jazmin rolls her eyes at the boring question, and she turns her back to him.

Complete freeze-out. My heart sinks.

"It's like a car accident in slow motion," I say. "We have to save him."

"Right. Let's go!" Daisy says.

We rush across the room, but before we can get to him, Ishaan jumps back, his face flush with embarrassment, and he hurries away, disappearing into the crowd.

"He's gonna be crushed," I say.

"We'll talk to him on the walk home," Daisy says.

I should go and look for him, but with Daisy on my arm, I don't want to go anywhere. Plus, the beer is starting to taste good. I take a swig and realize my second bottle is empty.

"Wow, you're drinking like a pro," Daisy says.

"I'm good with liquids. And solids, come to think of it. And now I'm in the mood for another one."

She looks at me uncertainly.

"You're the one who told me to taste it in the first place," I complain.

"Hey, I'm not trying to get between anyone and their party."

I look around the room for another beer, and I see Mia standing by a food table, a plate of uneaten sushi in her hands. I know her well enough to know she's miserable.

I begged my friends to come to a party with me. Now Ishaan is missing in action, and Mia looks like she did last year when her cat got diagnosed with IBS.

"Are you okay?" Daisy asks.

"I'm afraid my friends aren't having a good time."

"Based on what?"

"Based on the fact they look like they're at a funeral."

"Are you their babysitter?"

"Kind of. I mean no, but yes."

"More important—are you having a good time?"

"I'm having a good time with you," I say.

She smiles, and a tingle passes through my chest.

"Let's get you another beer and keep the party rolling," she says.

"Daisy Luna! Another great idea!"

I'm starting to sound drunk even to myself.

Before I can take a step, Ishaan appears in front of me, his face tense.

"It's been real," he says.

"You doing okay?" I ask. "I saw—"

"What did you see?" He grits his teeth.

"Nothing," I say, wanting to save him a little dignity.

"Anyway, I gotta get home and practice before my violin lesson tomorrow."

"You take lessons on Sunday?" Daisy asks.

"Doesn't everyone?" Ishaan asks, and he buttons his coat.

I turn to see Harry coming toward us.

"You taking off?" he asks me.

"No, my friend is," I say, pointing to Ishaan.

"Dude, brutal!" Harry says to Ishaan. "I saw you take your shot with Jazmin."

"I didn't take…" Ishaan says, his denial fizzling in mid-sentence.

"Hip-hop dancer and cheerleader," Harry says. "You're punching way above your weight class, little man."

Ishaan's face tightens. I know that look too well.

"We were just talking," Ishaan mumbles.

"Yeah, like six words," Harry says. "I'm not trying to be cruel, but—facts." Harry looks at me to back him up, but I keep my expression neutral.

Harry registers the tension, but he's not interested.

"Whatever. Have a good night, party people," Harry says before disappearing into the crowd.

I feel bad for Ishaan, but I don't know what to say. Just then we're interrupted by Mia rushing over with her jacket already on.

"You're leaving, too?"

"I'm done," she says. "I've had enough football party to last me for the rest of my life."

I'm a little annoyed that they want to run off so quickly. I look from them back to Daisy. No way I'm giving up on this party when it's going so well.

"If you have to leave, you have to leave," I tell Mia.

Mia wrinkles her nose. "So you're staying?"

"Um…" I look back toward Daisy.

She picks up on my discomfort. "Why don't we all hang together for the rest of the party and have some fun?" Daisy says. I like that she's trying to help my friends.

"Thanks but no thanks," Mia says.

"Fun?" Ishaan says. "This is like *Lord of the Flies* with Grubhub."

"Okay then," I say. "Get home safe."

Mia and Ishaan head for the door. They're not exactly running, but they're definitely speed-walking.

"Are they always like this?" Daisy asks.

"Pretty much. They have a selective idea of fun. They prefer it with a Sondheim score."

"What about you?"

"I have an ever-expanding idea of fun. And a new appreciation for beer."

"How many have you had?" she says with a grin.

Warmth spreads up my neck and into my cheeks. I close my eyes and lift my face toward the ceiling.

"Maximum two." Or was it three? I can't seem to remember.

I glance across the room and see Harry dancing with Jazmin. It's so easy for him, and so hard for guys like Ishaan and me. I feel anger flare in my chest, but I'm pulled back by Daisy's voice.

"Do you want to dance?" she asks.

"Dance?" I ask, stalling for time.

I look at Harry dancing again. It's like watching muscles in motion. I can't compete with that.

"I'm more a professional leaner," I tell Daisy.

"A professional what now?"

I strike a dramatic pose against the wall, leaning with a faux James Bond intensity.

"This, my dear Daisy, is the art of leaning. Few have mastered it."

"Impressive," she says. "But tonight you're going to learn a new art. The art of dancing."

She pulls me toward the dance floor. I resist, my eyes narrowing.

"People like me don't dance," I blurt out.

"People like you?"

Heat blooms in my cheeks. I can't tell if it's from self-consciousness or alcohol. Probably both.

"People who are— I'm just saying I'm not up for becoming a meme right now."

She laughs, still thinking I'm joking. "You afraid of going viral?"

"It's called DWO," I say. "Dancing While Overweight. No thank you."

Her face suddenly turns serious. "I'm sorry, but that is complete crap. There's no size limit. Anyone can dance. What about Lizzo?"

"She's amazing, but are there ten of her? There's only one, and everyone talks about how 'brave' she is. It's insulting if you really think about it."

"I'm not trying to tell you how to live your life, but we're in a body positive culture, and you're kind of negative."

"Only about myself," I say.

"So that's how it is? The world moves on and you stay stuck."

I sigh, frustrated. I wasn't planning to have this conversation with Daisy. Now or ever. But here we are.

"The world is talking about self-acceptance and body positivity," I say. "Meanwhile there's a blockbuster weight loss drug that keeps selling out because they can't manufacture enough of it. Kind of a mixed message, right?"

"Maybe I should mind my own business next time," Daisy says. "It's not my world, so who cares what I think?"

"You don't have to apologize. I know you're trying to help. I was just being real with you."

She nods, her tone softening. "Do you think about this stuff a lot?"

"Sometimes it seems like the only thing I think about."

Does beer make you tell the truth? Because I just told a whole lot more truth than I intended.

I'm expecting Daisy to make an excuse and drift away. Instead, she comes closer.

"I have a dumb idea. Maybe you could think about me instead."

"Like a distraction?"

Daisy grins. "Do I distract you, Eugene?"

She puts her hands on my shoulders and leans in, her face close to mine. She presses herself against me, and the breath catches in my chest.

"I'm not about forcing anyone to dance if they don't want to," she says, swaying in front of me. "But I guarantee you're not going to be a meme tonight if you decide to have some fun with me."

I don't know if it's the night, the beer, or Daisy—but I start to dance. My body is stiff, my movements clunky. But Daisy takes the lead, rocking in time to the music with her arms in mine, prompting me, her words soft and encouraging. I close my eyes and let the music take me. I open them again to find Daisy's eyes fixed on mine, a smile playing on her lips. The world narrows down to just us two, swaying to the rhythm, lost in the moment. Around us, people are dancing, laughing, having a great time.

For once I'm not thinking about myself. I'm just having fun.

"Not so bad, right?" she asks.

"Not bad at all."

A particularly loud cheer erupts from a group nearby, jolting me back to reality. I stumble slightly, out of rhythm, the ever-present self-consciousness creeping in. But Daisy's grip tightens around my hand, anchoring me.

"You're doing great, Eugene. Just keep looking at me," she says, her voice filled with encouragement.

I focus on Daisy, on the warmth of her hand in mine, on the light in her eyes, on the soft sway of her body. And for the first time in my life, I'm not a guy leaning against a wall, worrying about how he looks and if he fits in. I'm dancing.

I look over and catch Harry's attention. He's dancing with two beautiful girls at the same time, and he gives me a silent thumbs-up, then turns his attention back to his partners.

Daisy breaks contact, and I look over, startled.

"Bathroom," she mouths, and she dances away across the room.

With Daisy gone, my confidence does a nosedive. It's definitely time for another beer.

I weave through the party, the beat of the music pounding in my ears, and the warm haze of alcohol making everything feel a little distant.

I've barely stepped into the kitchen when a hand suddenly clamps onto my shoulder, pulling me to a stop. I turn, and there he is—Dillon, eyes dark and focused solely on me.

"How'd you get here?" Dillon's voice is low and menacing, and I smell the alcohol wafting off him.

"Harry invited me," I say.

"It's cool that he invited his mascot."

"I'm on the team, just like you," I say.

"You're nothing like me," he sneers.

"What's your problem with me, Dillon? You've been a jerk since freshman year."

"You're a quitter," he says. "I can smell it a mile away, mixed with the odor of chocolate chip cookies."

"The fat jokes are getting old, dude."

But it's not the fat stuff that gets to me tonight. It's the quitter part.

I quit writing the play last summer. I tried to quit football before Harry talked me back in. Maybe he's right and I'm a quitter.

Then I look in his eyes. Who the hell is he to tell me these things? Rage surges inside me, just like when I ran at that tackle dummy.

"I don't know anything about football," I say, leaning in and lowering my voice. "But it seems like if the offensive line were good enough, Harry wouldn't have begged some new guy to join the team."

Dillon squints with anger. He puffs out his chest, his face inches from mine. It's like he's daring me to take a swing. Even with a couple beers in me, I'm not dumb enough to make a move.

He reaches out with one hand, almost in slow motion, until his palm is against my chest. Then he pushes me. It's not a violent push, but it's a surprise, and I step back.

"Pudge Don't Budge," he says with a sneer. "We'll see about that."

I close my eyes against the shame I feel. When I open them again, he's gone. The volume rises on the party, the thumping beats vibrating through the floor and the sound of kids laughing in the other room.

I rush back through the crowd. Daisy intercepts me near the front door.

"Wait—where are you going?"

"I have to take off," I say.

"I thought we were staying. Did something happen while I was gone?"

I feel the afterburn of shame from talking with Dillon. The party rages on behind us—laughter, shouts, music. Daisy pauses, her gaze lingering over the crowd.

"Stay if you want to," I say. "But I should probably go."

"No way. I'll come with you," she says, and she reaches for my hand.

CHAPTER TWENTY-THREE:
CLOSE ENCOUNTERS ON
SEVENTY-FOURTH STREET

Daisy and I stand outside the party, the night air thick with the scent of trees from Central Park. The city hums around us—doormen chattering, cabs rumbling by on the avenue, and the clip-clop of horse hooves from the old-fashioned buggies. We face each other, the familiar awkwardness hanging in the air. This is the moment I've seen in countless plays and movies—the moment before the first kiss.

I lean in, then I stop suddenly. I'm thinking about Dillon when I should be thinking about Daisy. What if he was right? What if I don't belong here?

I take an involuntary step back.

"Are you in your head again?" Daisy asks.

"Maybe," I say, studying my shoes. "I haven't done much kissing."

"Is that a humblebrag?"

"No, it's reality."

She holds a finger to her lips, gently silencing me.

"It's not so difficult," she says.

She takes my arm and leads me away from the streetlight into the shadows of a red brick building. I put my hands on the wall.

"Did you want to see me lean again?" I ask.

"No more jokes," she says. She smiles, waiting.

I gather my courage, lean in, and I kiss her.

Our lips meet, warm and gentle, and the world fades away.

It feels like it lasts forever, but eventually we come up for air.

"That was—wow," I say.

"A playwright at a loss for words. Kind of nice."

"I've lost entire sentences," I say.

"What do you mean?"

"Writing plays is harder than I realized," I say.

"You want to talk about plays right now?"

I look at Daisy, her eyes twinkling in the glow of the streetlights.

"Not really," I say. "I'd rather talk about you and me."

"What do you want to talk about?"

"Your lips."

"Excellent choice," she says, and we kiss again.

She steps back and sighs. "That was a perfect ending to a perfect night."

We walk together, our fingers entwined and our footsteps in perfect rhythm. When we get to Seventy-Second and Broadway, Daisy lets go of my hand, and I immediately feel the loss.

"I'm gonna grab the subway to head uptown," she says.

"Hey, before you go—"

She stops and looks back.

"Why me?" I ask. "I mean, you could be with a lot of guys. So why me?"

She shrugs. "I feel like you really see me. And I like that feeling."

I smile, warmth spreading across my chest despite the cool night air.

"Good night, Daisy Luna."

"No," she says with a smile. "We say *nos vemos*. See you soon."

I want to ask her if soon could be tomorrow, but that's probably a mistake.

She waves and heads toward the subway. As I watch her go, I think about what Manny Cruz told me in the park, that making a fool out of yourself in front of a girl is the way all great love stories begin.

Tonight I drank, I danced, and I made terrible jokes—and the night still ended with a kiss.

But what if I screw it up the next time?

CHAPTER TWENTY-FOUR:
THE BIGGER MAN

Our first kiss was Saturday night. Fireworks and everything. I spent all of Sunday replaying the moment and dreaming about seeing Daisy again in school on Monday. But now that it's Monday morning, I'm walking down the hall in a semi-panic because I have no idea how to act when I see her. Do I rush over and kiss her, or play it cool and wait for her to come to me, or what exactly?

Wabash passes by and does a double take.

"*The minutes seem like hours,*" Wabash says.

"Huh?"

"You were singing 'Tonight.' The song from *West Side Story*?" he says.

"I didn't realize I was singing. I guess I'm happy," I say, a little surprised at myself. I mean, who's happy in school on a Monday morning?

"Any particular reason for your joie de vivre?" Wabash asks.

"I was working on the play over the weekend."

"Our play?" he asks excitedly. "Do tell."

"I was living out some scenes from it. The romantic scenes. This week I'll write them down."

He smiles. "I like your form of inspiration. Let me know if I can help with the writing."

Wabash starts to walk away, and I stop him.

"Can I ask you something awkward?"

"My dramaturgical services extend to the awkward," he says.

"I kissed this girl," I say. "And I don't know what to do when I see her."

"As a master of the romantic arts," Wabash says, "I advise you to play it cool. That's what worked with my former beau. I laid down a trail of breadcrumbs and let him find his way back to yours truly."

"I'm not following."

"Let the girl come to you," Wabash says.

"But what if she doesn't?"

"Confidence, m'lad."

I look around the hall, and every guy suddenly seems better looking than me, better dressed, and more in shape. The old doubts come rushing in. What chance do I really have with Daisy?

"Confidence isn't really my thing," I tell Wabash. "I'm more about discomfort."

"Discomfort?" he asks.

We pause in the doorway outside an empty classroom, and I lower my voice.

"Because I'm bigger than other people."

"Ah... You're self-conscious."

"I guess. Yeah."

He nods. "I know it well. Been there, done that, designed a hat for it."

"Do you ever—I mean, the gender-nonconforming thing—"

"What about it?"

"Do you ever feel different?"

He thinks about it for a second. "Most of the time, Guterman. But do you know what else I feel? Freedom. To be myself."

"That's how I felt Saturday night," I say. "I was drunk, so maybe it doesn't count."

"Maybe it was a taste of what's to come," Wabash says. "Not the drunk part. But the freedom."

"Maybe."

"Awkward moment concluded. I bid you adieu," Wabash says, and he bows and continues on his way.

CHAPTER TWENTY-FIVE:
JEALOUSY MODE ACTIVATED

When I walk into the computer room, my good feelings take a nosedive. Mia is munching on baby carrots and scowling at me.

"Didn't hear from you Sunday," she says.

"Were we supposed to do something?" I ask.

I spent most of Sunday in bed with a bottle of pain reliever, doing my best to hide a hangover from my mother.

"We were gonna do our fall foliage tour in the park," she says. "Like we do every year."

"Was that this weekend? I'm so sorry. I got distracted."

"You've been distracted a lot lately," she says.

"Hey, I got a big life," I say with a laugh.

I'm hoping to put an end to the conversation, but I only manage to irritate her.

She shakes her head and nibbles another carrot. The crunching sound is turning my little headache into a bigger one.

"How did the rest of the party go?" she asks, more than mildly curious.

"Fine."

"I heard a few rumors."

"What kinds of rumors?"

"I don't know. I don't listen to rumors. But you missed our walk, and you didn't touch base with Ishaan. He's kind of a mess, and I don't know why."

I do. He got rejected and had it rubbed in his face, and I didn't call him after.

"What's up, Mia? Why are you grilling me?"

"You dragged me to the worst party of my life, then disappeared. It's a little strange, Eugene."

Worst? How do I tell Mia it was the best party of my life?

"I don't want to fight," Mia says. "I just wanted to let you know I did my recon."

"Recon?"

"On that Daisy girl, remember?"

"I remember, but I don't need it anymore. You met her, right? You know she's cool."

"I met her, but I don't know her," Mia says. "And neither do you. You've barely known her for like a week. It takes longer than that to break in a new keyboard."

I take a deep breath, doing all I can not to blow up at Mia.

"So you don't want to know what I found out?" Mia asks.

"Give me the headlines," I say cautiously.

"She had to leave Philly."

"Right, because her family moved. She already told me."

"They didn't move *with* her. They moved because of her."

I'm surprised, but I try not to show it. "She said she had a little problem with alcohol."

"That's what she said, huh?"

Mia crunches down on a carrot, watching me closely. Of course I'm curious. How could I not be?

"What did you hear?" I finally ask.

"She got suspended for drinking on school property."

"That's pretty serious. But people make mistakes."

"Then it happened again. Only the second time, she wasn't alone."

"So she was drinking with a friend."

"A guy. And they were caught—shall we say—in a compromising position. And there's a video."

"Gross, Mia. You're better than this."

"I'm just passing along what the socials said."

"So the girl who's creating Authentic Social Media is repeating social media gossip?"

Mia's face turns red and she quickly turns away.

"Bottom line: I don't trust her," Mia says.

"You don't have to trust her because she's not your friend—I am."

"Are you really my friend?" she asks skeptically.

"Why would you ask that?"

"Because you're acting—I'm not sure who you are anymore," she says.

"I'm changing a little. I think it's called peaking."

I smile, hoping that's enough to placate her, but she's not having it.

"That's getting really tired," she says. "I want you to peak, too. This isn't how I saw it going."

"It's going great," I say.

"So you're working on your play?"

I tried to write after the party last night, but I drew a blank.

Mia angrily stuffs her half-eaten bag of carrots into her backpack. How can a person not even finish a bag of baby carrots?

"Maybe we need a little break from each other," she says abruptly. "I'm busy with my start-up, and you're busy with your girlfriend."

So that's what Mia is upset about. She must have heard that I kissed Daisy, and she's angry that I didn't tell her.

"For the record, she's not my girlfriend," I say.

"Crush, obsession, whatever," Mia says. "I've got things to do, and you've got different things, so—"

"So what are you saying?"

Mia chews her lower lip. "I'll see you around," she says.

"Yeah," I say, feeling a lump form in my throat. "See you."

She practically runs out of the room, slamming the door behind her.

CHAPTER TWENTY-SIX:
WELCOME TO THE A-TEAM

I stumble to the cafeteria for lunch, feeling disoriented from the lingering hangover and whatever happened with Mia. Plus I'm worried about Ishaan. Mia said he's messed up, and he hasn't texted me since before the party.

He's not at our usual table, but when I turn to leave, Langford intercepts me and beckons me over toward the football table, where the guys greet me.

I glance at Dillon, who barely gives me a nod. After our run-in at the party, I trust him even less than I did before.

"Pudge rocked it Saturday night," Langford announces.

"And it rocked me Sunday," I groan, rubbing my head. "Future reference. What do you do for a hangover?"

"You gotta drink more," Harry says. "Build up that tolerance."

"And you gotta hydrate," Langford says, and hands me a can of soda.

It's regular Coke—not diet—but I gratefully chug it back.

"Pull up some bench," Langford says.

After trash-talking me at practice, I thought Langford hated me, but now it seems like I passed some kind of test with him. He pushes a tray my way, offering me his cookie. I don't want these guys to have another reason to tease me, so I take a pass.

Harry scoots closer, and I look around, uncertain. I never sat at this table before, but I do my best to act casual. I don't know if I was expecting the bench to have extra padding or a massage function, but it's the same bench we sit on across the cafeteria. Only for whatever reason, this bench feels better.

"How long does a hangover last exactly?" I ask the table.

"Was it your first one?" Harry asks.

"Yeah," I admit.

"Yesterday was the worst," Langford says. "It'll only get better from here."

"What up, guys?" Jazmin says. She's stopped in front of the table with her two friends.

I flash back to the awful moment she turned away from Ishaan at the party.

"Great party, Harry," she says, totally attentive.

"For sure," he says with a nod, and he turns his attention back to his lunch tray.

Three of the most well-known girls in school are standing there trying to have a conversation, and Harry couldn't care less.

The girls laugh nervously before moving on.

"You're not going to talk to them?" I ask Harry.

He shrugs. "She's a cool girl. But I'm hungry."

"You can't conversate with every girl who walks by," Dillon says. "Not enough hours in the day."

I do my best not to do a cartoon jaw drop.

"You seen your girl today?" Harry asks. "She's looking hot."

The comment makes me uncomfortable, but the guys at the table perk right up.

"I don't have a girl," I say quietly.

"So who were you dancing with all night?" Dillon says with a laugh.

"A friend," I say.

"Friends don't get all dressed up on a Monday," Harry says.

"You think she got dressed up for me?"

"I don't know for sure," Harry says. "But I wouldn't be surprised."

I laugh with excitement at the possibility, but I get some strange looks, so I shut it down.

"I'm a fan of the ladies, but you gotta put the social life on ice while we practice," Harry says.

"No dating?"

"Who's got time for dating?" Dillon says. "Not during training."

Wait, what's going on here? Half the reason I agreed to football was because of Daisy. Now I'm not supposed to be with her?

"We go pretty hard," Harry says. "You'll see."

I don't want to see. Now I'm worried all over again about what I got myself into.

"I'm not saying you can't hang with your girl," Harry says. "Just put football first and everything else will find its place."

"I'd better get in line and grab some lunch," I announce before I hear something else I don't want to hear.

"Stay here and relax," Langford says. "I'll get you some chow."

He stands up like he's going to bring me my food.

"You don't have to do that," I say.

"It's not a 'have to.' It's a 'want to.'"

"We know how to take care of our own," Harry says. "And you're one of us now. Isn't that right, Dill?"

Dillon nods faintly. "Sure enough. We gotchu, Pudge!"

I hear it but I don't believe it. Especially not coming from him.

I sit back on the bench, and I take in the POV from the football table. The cafeteria used to be a war zone for me—being careful where I walked, only sitting in my usual seat, hyperaware of what food was on my tray and who saw me eating it. Now as I glance around the table at the football bros grinning and nodding at me, I'm starting to feel accepted.

Are they faking it like Dillon? Or just following Harry's commandments?

I don't know, but a guy could get used to this.

Just then Ishaan walks into the cafeteria alone. He sits at our usual table and takes out the bagged lunch his mom makes for him four days a week. I have to admit he looks pitiful all alone over there.

He glances up and sees me on the wrong side of the room, and his eyes grow wide. I've been eating with him and Mia for two years, but now I'm at the jocks' table. I want to go over to him, but I don't know how to handle the situation.

He doesn't wait. He stands and slowly comes over, leaving his food back at the table.

Before he can say anything, Langford returns and puts a lunch tray down in front of me. It's piled with food—a double burger with a side of fries, rice, and salad. Two big chocolate chip cookies hang off the end of the tray like magnificent rock formations.

Ishaan looks from the tray to me, unsure of what's going on.

"This is great," I tell Langford. "But I'm trying to do more salads."

"Salads are for the swim team," Langford says. "We're football players."

"That's right," Harry says. "You need to build muscle while keeping up your weight."

I would never normally eat so much food in public. That's like asking for someone to comment about my weight.

"You actually want me to eat what's on this tray? Right now?"

The jocks look from one to the other, unsure of why I'm even asking.

Ishaan clears his throat loudly, and I realize he's been standing there watching all this. I was so transfixed by the food, I forgot about him.

"Hey, how's it going?" I say nervously.

He takes in the table like they're old friends.

"What's up, dudes?" he says too loudly.

The entire table stares at him. "Who are you?" Langford asks.

"I was at the party Saturday night. Remember?"

"Nope," Dillon says.

"I remember," Harry says, and he makes a gesture of a plane falling out of the sky and crashing.

"Oh, you're that guy," Dillon says, triggering laughs around the table.

"Hey, he's my friend," I say, feeling uncomfortable.

"Can I talk to you?" Ishaan asks under his breath.

"Be right back," I announce, and I follow Ishaan and sit at our old familiar table in the corner of the cafeteria.

I settle onto the bench and look around. It's not my imagination. The cafeteria feels different from over here.

"You used to look down on those guys," Ishaan says. "Now it seems like you're one of them."

"Starting to be."

"I guess they're your new social group, too."

"It was a party, Ishaan. Not a lifetime commitment. And I seem to remember you getting excited when I invited you."

Ishaan shifts uncomfortably. "Yeah, well, there are a lot of things I'd like to forget about that night."

The image of Jazmin snubbing him comes to mind. "I'm sorry things went sideways with Jazmin."

"Who's Jazmin? I have no recollection of her."

"Come on, dude. Can we just talk about it?"

"I don't do feelings; I'm not Mia. Anyway, you can make your own life choices. I don't care."

"Look, I'm just trying to fit in. What's wrong with that?"

"I can try to fit my violin into a flute case, but guess what? It's still a violin."

"What does that mean?"

"I saw those guys up close and personal at the party, and you're not one of them."

"You don't know what I am," I say angrily.

Ishaan's face goes red. "Now I know what Mia was talking about," he mutters.

I sit up fast. "What did she tell you?"

"She said you're frenemies now."

"That's her choice, not mine."

"Well, something obviously happened," Ishaan says, "because she's texting me your name punctuated with rage-filled emojis."

"She thinks Daisy's a faker and I'm falling for it. Or something like that."

"Is she a faker?"

"You met her. What do you think?"

I realize I still care about Ishaan's opinion, even though it probably shouldn't matter.

"She seems cool," he says with a shrug.

I lean toward him. "We kissed," I say quietly.

"What?!"

I gesture for him to keep his voice down. "After the party. Mia doesn't even know."

"You had your first kiss?"

"It was more like my first baker's dozen."

"I don't believe it," Ishaan says, his face a mix of envy and excitement. "My boy has become a man."

"That happened at my bar mitzvah."

"The only thing you kissed at your bar mitzvah was the torah. This is next level."

I smile as I remember what it felt like to be with Daisy. "I guess you're right."

"And I'm the one who told you about Daisy in the first place," he says. "Credit where credit is due."

I look across the room at the football table, where an empty seat awaits me.

"You'd better get back," Ishaan says. "Looks like there's a big lunch tray with your name on it."

"Are we okay?" I ask.

"Hell, yeah. I'm not losing my best friend over this. Besides, I'm living vicariously through your lips right now."

I laugh and look back at the jock table.

I look down at my hands, feeling conflicted. "This is all happening really fast."

He studies me for a moment. "You know, I always figured you'd find your place eventually. I thought it would be on Broadway, not in a locker room with a bunch of sweaty guys."

"When you're as comfortable with your body as I am, you can't wait to change in front of strangers."

Ishaan laughs. "I'm glad your dreams are coming true," he says. "Just don't forget the little people who got you there."

CHAPTER TWENTY-SEVEN:
STRANGER DANGER

Once I commit to football, it more or less takes over my life. Harry wasn't kidding when he said we go hard. I'm on the field with him and the guys at least five times a week with workouts in between. Occasionally Coach schedules "two-a-days" where we have a practice before *and* after school on the same day. It's brutal, but the jocks don't even flinch.

"There's life in season and life out of season," Harry explains. "And we are definitely in season."

All I want to do is hang out with Daisy, but there's hardly any time. We go to dinner twice with a bunch of football guys and their dates, but our situationship stays a situation and doesn't become a relationship. Not as far as I can tell at least. We kiss goodbye once, but it's not the hot session we had after the party. Just a quick peck on the lips that leaves me confused and craving more.

And my friends? I tell myself I'm making time for them and nothing has really changed, but my life becomes football, sleep, and school.

Ice, rinse, and repeat.

One day I walk into study hall, and the first thing I see is Ishaan and Mia sharing a table in the corner. Mia's face is half hidden behind a massive stack of books, and she's flipping through pages like she's hunting for buried treasure. Ishaan's pecking at his laptop, visibly annoyed as usual. The sight of them both makes me smile.

"Got room for a third?" I ask.

A shushing sound from around the library answers before they do. Some kid across the room says "Keep it down" in a whisper so loud it's ridiculous.

Ishaan glances up, eyebrows raised. "What's up, stranger?"

"Stranger? When did I earn that title?" I say.

I sit down, but Mia won't even acknowledge my presence.

"Dude, you vanished," Ishaan says. "It's been a couple weeks."

"It doesn't feel that long."

"Well, it is. You ditched us."

I get a lump in my throat at being called out by Ishaan.

"I've been super busy with practice. Those football bros go hard. It's like being in nonstop tech."

Mia glances up at the mention of football, but she still doesn't say anything.

"That's who you are now? A football bro?" Ishaan asks.

"You say it like it's a bad thing. I'm the same me. I just got responsibilities."

"You're the same? Okay, then," Ishaan says, flipping his laptop closed. "Movie night tonight. You in?"

Mia raises an eyebrow. I feel a flicker of the old times along with the pressure to prove nothing is different between us.

"Why not?" I say. "A movie sounds great."

"You don't have practice?" Ishaan asks.

"Not on Friday nights. In the morning."

"You're coming, right, Mia?" Ishaan asks.

She eyes me skeptically. "Fine. But only if Eugene is really going."

I'm relieved that Mia hasn't totally shut me out.

"So do we fight over the movie like the old days," I ask, "or are you working your way through a franchise?"

"Mia doesn't do franchise movies—remember?"

"I do limited series," Mia protests.

My phone buzzes. A text from Harry. *Workout tonight. You and me.*

An invite from Harry. Not mandatory. But he's never asked me to work out one-on-one before. I wonder what he wants?

I look back at Ishaan. "Hey, this is awkward, but I totally forgot I have something tonight."

"Oh, now you have something?" Ishaan says. "That's some serious bait and switch."

"Don't waste your energy," Mia says. "He probably has a date."

"It's not a date," I say, though I wish it was. "We'll do it next Friday. I swear. I'll make it up to you."

Ishaan's eyes grow cold. "Nothing to make up," Ishaan says. "Do your thing. I don't hold friends back."

My phone buzzes again, a question mark from Harry. I send him a quick thumbs-up.

"You guys are the best," I say, and I slip out of study hall, not wanting to see the look on my friends' faces.

CHAPTER TWENTY-EIGHT:
THE TRAINING GROUND

Harry slaps a forty-five-pound plate onto the barbell. "All right, Pudge, next one is the deadlift. It hits every muscle you need on the field."

"I didn't even know I had muscles until two weeks ago. I mean, I knew they were there, but I never used them."

Harry chuckles and points to the bar. "Let's do it, bro."

I look around Harry's high-end fitness club on Columbus Avenue in the Seventies. There's a whole world in here—pool, weight training, treadmills and bikes, massage rooms, yoga spaces. Basically, my idea of hell. But they do have their own restaurant. I wish I was there right now, but I force my attention back on Harry and the training.

I grip the bar, recalling the cues: shoulders back, lift with the legs. The barbell comes off the ground, my body straightening until I lock out at the top.

"Nice. Lower it down, controlled. Again."

"I don't hang out in gyms much," I say.

"Where do you hang?"

"Donut Prince."

"I can't do donuts during the season. I got a whole nutrition plan."

"That sucks."

"Not really. I got places to go, and I gotta keep it tight. And this arm is—or was—going to take me there."

I look at his cast, filled with guilt. "But it's healing, right?"

"We'll know more in a few weeks."

He picks up a kettlebell with his good arm, curling it as he talks to me.

"There aren't enough Arab American players in football, you know? I want to change that. So I'm going for it, hard."

"It's like your dream."

"Hell no, it's my reality. College ball, then get my shot at the pros." He puts down the kettlebell. "What about you?"

"I want my plays to be on Broadway."

"Want to?"

"It's kind of a long shot."

"Bro, you're killing me with all the doubts. How about cut the crap and just go for it?"

"Maybe, yeah."

I try a couple more reps, but the bar is getting heavier with every lift. I don't want to look like a quitter in front of Harry, so I step back and stretch like I pulled a muscle.

"Speaking of going for it," Harry says. "What's the deal with you and Daisy? You guys still talking?"

"It's weird. We were connecting, but since practice got serious, we haven't seen much of each other."

Harry laughs. "You're overthinking it, man. Surprise her somehow. Girls like it when you're spontaneous."

"What if she thinks I'm weird?"

161

"You kissed her, right?"

"Yeah, but that was a couple weeks ago."

"So you're already past the weird part. You gotta advance the ball downfield."

"Advance the ball—"

"You're either moving toward the goal or you're losing. That's how the game works."

"The love game or football?"

"Is there a difference?" he says, and he tosses me a towel.

CHAPTER TWENTY-NINE: RISKY BUSINESS

As I'm leaving the gym, I look up and see the street sign—Seventy-Fourth Street. I'm a block away from where I kissed Daisy for the first time. A wave of loneliness washes over me. How can a person be lonelier after meeting someone than they were beforehand? It's like now that I know what it's like to be with her, it's painful to be without her.

But then I think of what Harry said about advancing the ball.

I look at my phone, and I realize it's only a little past eight. My finger hovers over my phone screen, ready to text Daisy. But what do I say? Harry would just type *'Sup?* And he'd probably be in bed with a woman six minutes later.

But I'm not a *'Sup* kind of guy. After taking a deep breath, I settle on:

It's Eugene, what are you up to?

A few seconds pass, and the reply comes:

Who is this?

I panic, wondering if I got the number wrong. Seconds pass in silence until I get another text:

j/k. I know who it is

Wow. Way to give a guy a heart attack.

Okay, then. It's time to take a chance.

In your hood. Wanna take a walk?

Three blinking dots seem to last for eternity, until she finally types back:

Sure.

I'm not really in her neighborhood, but I'm a couple stops away, so I race for the subway and grab the local uptown.

⊙⊙⊙

Twenty minutes later she walks around the corner; her hair is in a baseball cap, and she's wearing a jean jacket and black leggings. Seeing her again takes my breath away, and I have to remind myself to play it cool.

"You just happened to be in my neighborhood?" she asks.

"Harry and I were hanging out."

"Your best bud, Harry," she says.

"Something like that."

"I haven't seen you much."

"Football—who knew? It's like I married my helmet and nobody told me."

"I get it."

"I keep wanting to call you, but—"

"No, it's okay," she says too quickly.

There's an ache in my chest. All I've wanted is to spend time with Daisy, but the football commitment is relentless.

"You have a little time now?" I ask.

She smiles sweetly. "Sure."

Daisy and I set off walking side by side without saying anything at first, until we reach an empty bench just outside Riverside Park, surrounded by trees and glowing streetlights.

I lean in for the possibility of a kiss, but she's bent over tying her sneaker, and I find myself hovering in the air waiting for her to finish. I quickly lean back on the bench, clearing my throat and pretending it didn't just happen.

"So tell me everything," she says when she sits back up.

"I'm good," I say. "Actually, that's a lie. Things are complicated."

"Like what things?"

"Let's see— My friends are angry at me, I'm not writing, I'm doing football all the time, and my mom's still giving me crap about my weight—"

"That's a lot of things."

"You don't want to hear all this," I say, suddenly embarrassed.

"I do want to hear it," she says. "But is that why you texted me? You needed a friend to talk to?"

"That and—"

"And what?" she asks.

I feel that tingle in my chest, just like the first time we talked.

"I've been thinking about you," I say.

"I've been thinking about you, too."

Our eyes meet, but neither of us makes a move. I remember what Wabash said. *Let the girl come to you.*

"It's weird to see each other in school, right?" I ask.

"A little."

"I don't know how to act around you."

"How do you want to act?"

"I want to be closer to you."

"You're closer now."

I wait, holding my breath—

She scoots toward me until our shoulders touch. We sit together, side by side on the bench, her body warm next to mine.

"I couldn't wait to see you again," I say.

"Just see me?"

"And kiss you." I'm barely able to get the words out.

Daisy reaches up and lightly strokes my cheek.

"Well, what are you waiting for?" she asks.

She's right. I stop waiting.

CHAPTER THIRTY:
FIRST DOWNS AND FOOTBALL CLOWNS

I step onto the turf at Randall's Island Park. A green battlefield so close to Manhattan, yet a world away.

Practice is over. It's time for my first varsity game.

A month ago, walking onto a football field was on my top ten list of things to avoid. But a few weeks of nonstop practices combined with Harry's mentorship has me feeling like I belong here. Almost.

I pull at my uniform, uncomfortable at the tight fit, especially now that I'm wearing it in public.

I glance at the stands. Daisy sits there, a bright spot among the cheering football fans who are strangers to me. And then there's Ishaan with someone next to him— It's Mia! A jolt of surprise. I didn't expect either of them to be here. We've barely spoken a word to each other since that day in study hall, and seeing Mia brings up a pang as I realize I miss her. The two of them couldn't look more out of place, but they're here, supporting me.

I pull at the uniform again. I wonder if I should have ordered a larger size...

"Focus, Pudge," Harry says. I wince a little at the name, but it brings me back to the present moment.

Our main rivals, the Holy Cross football team, jog onto the field like they mean business.

"This is where it gets real," Harry says.

"Real painful," I mutter, anticipating the battle to come.

After the kickoff, I take the field with my teammates, and I gaze into the face of a mountain of a man, the defensive lineman standing across from me, the word *TANK* printed across the front of his helmet.

"What's Tank?"

"It's me. Last name Stankevic."

"Why don't they call you Stank?"

"Because I will hurt them, and they know it. What do they call you?"

"Pudge."

"To your face?"

"It's like a cool nickname."

"I don't think so."

I sense Harry behind me, his energy intense, and I take my stance.

"Hut! Hut! Hike!" Harry calls, and the ball is snapped.

Tank charges like a battering ram. In seconds, I'm flat on my back, staring up into his menacing face.

Langford steps in, side-checking the guy and helping me up. I glance at Daisy and feel ashamed. Then I see Mia and Ishaan with concern on their faces.

"Don't let him get in your head," Langford says. "Get into his."

"He's not in my head. He's crashing into my body."

Langford grins. "You got this, bro. Dig deep."

I take a deep breath as I head back to the line. Am I Pudge the weak link? Or am I Pudge, the wall that can't be breached?

I step up to the line, grunting as I kick the turf. Tank's eyes narrow, but there's a flicker of uncertainty.

"'Sup, Stank?"

His jaw tightens. "Nobody calls me Stank."

"Based on the smell, I'd say it's what they're thinking."

On Harry's call, I blast off the line. The surge of power takes Tank by surprise, and his steps falter. He crashes into me, but it's weak, uncoordinated. Harry easily passes over our heads, and the crowd erupts.

I look at Tank, struggling to regain his balance. "You need to take a breather, Stank? Maybe hit the showers early? I could recommend a deodorant soap."

"You talk too much."

"It's a gift."

He looks angry, but I can tell my words are getting to him. I'm in his head, just like Langford taught me.

Harry calls the next play, and I brace myself, arms up, eyes locked on Tank. But he fakes left, darts right. My balance tips and I'm down, face mask grinding into the turf.

I turn, heart plummeting, as Tank scurries past me, a speeding train directed at Harry. He played me, feigning upset. But he's running like a guy on a mission. The worst-case scenario flashes in my mind: Harry's fractured wrist breaking again under the force of the impact.

Then like a bolt of lightning, Dillon comes out of nowhere, slamming into Tank, the two of them tumbling down in a sprawl of grunts and flailing limbs.

Harry's pass sails through the air, untouched. He turns, taking in the scene. Me out of position and on all fours, Tank at his feet, pinned beneath Dillon.

He's safe. No thanks to me.

Dillon and Harry high-five, then Harry's eyes meet mine.

No words, just a frown of disappointment that makes me feel like I've let the whole team down.

CHAPTER THIRTY-ONE:
FRENEMIES REUNITED

Mia and Ishaan are waiting for me after the game. Ishaan has his violin strapped to his back, and Mia's hair color is back to what it was last year. It makes me smile to see them.

"Someone planned a reunion and didn't let me know," I say with a grin.

"Ishaan told me about the game," Mia says. "And I thought you could use a mascot."

She makes a half-hearted motion like a dancing cat, and I laugh.

"I'm surprised you both came. How'd you like the game?"

"Football? It's violent," Mia says.

"No kidding. You should see my black-and-blue marks." I start to lift my pant leg.

"I'll take a hard pass on that," Ishaan says with a laugh.

"But you were great, Eugene," Mia says.

I look over to see Daisy walking down the stairs with some friends. She gives me a half wave, and I smile in her direction.

"Did you hear me?" Mia asks, her eyes tracking mine to Daisy.

"Huh?" I say, turning back to her.

"I said you did great out there—it looked like you really knew what you were doing."

"Right, until the end when I totally blew it."

"Puuuuuuudge!" Langford shouts, punching me in the shoulder as he passes by.

"I don't like when they call you that," Mia says, her face tightening.

"It's a term of affection."

"It doesn't sound affectionate to me."

"Did you come all the way to Randall's Island to criticize my new life?"

"Hold on," Ishaan says. "Before you guys go there, Mia has something she wants to say, right?"

Mia sighs. "Okay, look, I've been a jerk," she says. "I said things I shouldn't have, and I'm sorry. I guess I was a little jealous of your new friends."

The apology isn't Mia's style, which makes it even more significant. "I appreciate it," I say.

"What I meant to say earlier: football is...whatever. No matter what happens, there's always a way back to us."

"We didn't discuss that last part," Ishaan says.

"You're saying I could come back to you. Like I'm lost?" I snap.

Ishaan tries to play peacemaker. "Mia means we got your back."

It's insulting. "I've got an entire team who has my back," I say. "Why do I need you two?"

The air between us chills over.

"Nice to see you fit in somewhere, because you were obviously faking it with us," Mia says.

"I wasn't faking."

"Really? Because you used to be a theater person and our best friend. What are you now?"

"I'm popular," I say.

"Go to hell, Eugene."

"That's enough," Ishaan warns Mia.

"You know what, Mia? Enjoy your little venture into the world of start-ups," I say angrily. "I hope it makes you less cynical, but I doubt it."

"Our friendship—if we ever had one—is over," Mia says.

Her eyes darken, and she storms off.

I whip around to Ishaan, my rage boiling over. "And what about you? You have anything you want to get off your chest?"

He holds up his hands in protest. "Hell, dude, you're weirding me out. You got roid rage or something?"

The comment pulls me up short. Football has taught me to fight, but maybe I've learned the lesson a little too well.

I take a breath.

"I'm fine," I say. "Just sick of having to justify myself to her."

"Got it," Ishaan says. "No more justifying."

"Anyway, thanks for coming to the game."

"Yeah," Ishaan says, shaking his head. "So much for the reunion."

CHAPTER THIRTY-TWO:
QUITTERS NEVER WIN

I walk into the locker room after the game. I'm late getting back because of the toxic exchange with Mia, and now the room is buzzing. Muscles gleam, towels snap, and the testosterone flows. It's a parallel universe—

But after talking with Mia and Ishaan, I feel like an alien all over again.

I've mostly sidestepped changing in the locker room at school for the last couple weeks. I extend my time on the field after practice, pretending to get in some extra laps, or saying I have an errand and I'll shower at home. But today, at a strange locker room facility with Coach's post-game sermon on the horizon, there's no escape. So I'm stuck.

"Harry, got a sec?" I ask.

"Sure," he says. He peels off his jersey to reveal a torso that looks like it was carved from granite. "You gonna change?" he asks, grabbing for a towel.

"My mom says I'm perfect just the way I am."

"This kid is hilarious," Harry says, stepping out of his jockstrap.

Dear God, how much can I take in one day?

"So what happened out there?" Harry asks.

I strategically delay until he's swathed in a towel. "No way around it," I say. "I screwed up on that last play."

"You mean when you missed the block?" Harry asks.

"Yeah. I thought I got into Tank's head. But he faked me out somehow."

"It happens." Harry shrugs, tying a plastic bag around his cast.

As if on cue, Dillon strides by. "Saved your ass, bro. You can thank me later."

"But I had one job," I tell Harry. "To protect you."

"Did you go down on purpose?" Harry asks.

"Of course not."

"Then you live and you learn."

I can't believe it. These guys are so tough, but their reaction is the opposite of what I thought it would be. I flash back to other failures I've had, like the aftermath of last year's play festival, after which I hid from writing for six months.

"I thought if you fail at something, you should probably quit," I say.

"Quitters never win and winners never quit," Harry says.

"Is there a sports expression for every situation?" I chuckle.

"Pretty much," Harry agrees, heading toward the showers. "We're grabbing food after Coach's post-game. Bring Daisy if you want."

"Why would I bring her?"

"Because she's your girl, right?"

"Not exactly."

"I saw her out there. Watching you," he says. "Don't sleep on that. My experience, they don't watch forever."

CHAPTER THIRTY-THREE:
THE WORLD WAS WIDE ENOUGH

"Surprise!" Mom says, grinning and hiding something behind her back. She whips out an envelope. "Happy early birthday."

I eye the envelope cautiously.

"Who's in the mood for some Broadway?" Mom says giddily.

I rip the envelope and find two theater tickets. "*Hamilton?*"

"It's a musical," Mom says.

"I'm aware," I say dryly. Because I saw it three times with Dad before he moved out. "But you hate Broadway. Especially musicals."

"I don't hate them," she says. "Your dad used to try to drag me to Broadway all the time. Nobody likes to be dragged."

"Good point. But you're okay going to Broadway now?"

"I'll make an exception for my son. Also it's the hottest show in town."

"I think it was the hottest show of 2015."

"Then it's a classic now."

"Is this some kind of parent-child bonding maneuver?"

"You say that like it's a bad thing."

I sigh, taking a moment before I decide.

"Okay, I'm not turning down *Hamilton* tickets," I say.

Mom's face brightens. "How's school?"

She shifts topics, apparently trying to extend the good vibes.

"Can we not?" I ask.

"But I'm interested. What's up with your classes, how's your writing, what's happening with the theater club, are there any girls—"

"Thanks, but I have a previously scheduled interrogation I have to get to."

Mom holds up her hands in surrender. "Fine," she says.

She eyes me up and down. "You lost a little weight playing football," she says abruptly.

"Wow, Mom. Body shaming?"

"It's a compliment!"

"It's focusing on looks."

"It's not looks. I'm a medical doctor trained at Brigham and Women's Hospital," she defends herself, "and I'm worried about your health."

"You're obsessed with my body and it's inappropriate."

"I don't know how we got here from a compliment," Mom says, exasperated.

"Maybe if you trained at Brigham and *Men's* Hospital you'd get it," I shout, and I storm out.

"There's no such thing as Brigham and Men's!" she shouts back.

"Read the room!" I yell, and I slam my door.

A few seconds pass, and I hear her calling faintly from the living room.

"Are we still going to *Hamilton*?"

"Yeah," I scream, and I bury my face in my pillow.

CHAPTER THIRTY-FOUR:
DAISY'S GIFT

Daisy and I are leaving my birthday dinner at Playa Betty's restaurant, one of my favorite Upper West Side places. We've been out a few times since our kiss three weeks ago, but it's mostly been in groups. So being at a dinner date with just the two of us—and on my birthday weekend—feels like an upgrade.

"So what do you want for your birthday?" Daisy asks.

"I already have what I want," I say, channeling Mr. Romantic.

Daisy rolls her eyes. "That is cheesy and really sweet at the same time."

"But mostly sweet, right?"

She laughs. "You're so innocent. I kind of like that about you."

"What would be the non-innocent request for my birthday?"

She raises an eyebrow. "What most guys would ask for."

"Which is what?"

"Oral."

"Oral? Oh, that oral," I say, my face getting hot.

She laughs delightedly and takes my hand. "Come on, let's get you a birthday present."

She drags me down Broadway for a block or two, then turns abruptly and pulls me into an H&M department store.

I immediately tense up, pulling my hand away from hers.

"This place isn't for me," I say.

"Why?"

"They don't make my size," I admit, almost whispering.

"Wait—what?" Daisy asks.

"I'm too big to shop in a regular store."

The reality I've hidden for years is suddenly out in the open. I think about my argument with Mom last night. I accused her of being obsessed with weight, but I'm obsessed about it, too. The world's obsessed about it. Even people who pretend it's not a thing know that it's a thing, or else why would they be talking about it so much?

"I'm sorry," Daisy says. "I dragged you in here thinking it would be fun, and it didn't occur to me—"

"It's okay. It's not something average-sized people think about."

"Average-sized. Nobody ever called me that before."

"No offense. But it's a limited POV, y'know?"

"So you can't buy clothes in regular stores? That's like discrimination."

I shrug. "It is what it is. I get it. It's not like they can carry every size."

Daisy looks heartbroken but recovers quickly. "Let's try to find something. A fun experiment."

"I don't think it will be much fun for me."

"I love shopping, and I'm really, really good at it. I mean, like, next-level good. Maybe I can find something for you. Let me try, and if we don't, we don't."

If it were up to me, I'd be out of here in a second, but she's so excited about the idea...

"I should have asked for oral," I say.

"So you'll do it!" she says excitedly, and pulls me toward the men's section.

She stops suddenly, looking me up and down.

"What's your size?"

I look at my feet. The truth is I don't know exactly because I avoid clothes shopping like the plague.

"Take XL and multiply it by a couple XLs," I say, embarrassed.

"Okay," she says casually. "We can work with that. Don't go anywhere."

Daisy bolts, then returns barely two minutes later with a heap of clothes.

"Two looks," she says. "Look one is cowboy chic—"

A corduroy jacket with a white furry lining catches my eye. It's not something I'd buy for myself, but in Daisy's arms, it looks right.

"And look two—more of a rugged layered thing."

Daisy holds up a giant sweatshirt and lays a vest over it.

"I like them both," I say. "They're just too cool for me."

"Too cool for the Donut Prince? Not a chance."

She helps me slip into the corduroy jacket. To my surprise, it fits.

"Is it too tight?" I ask nervously.

"It looks amazing," she says, reassuring me with a smile.

"Okay then, I'm getting it."

"Great! And I'm gifting it to you—no arguments allowed."

"You don't have to buy me a gift."

"Not have to. Want to. You helped me adjust to a new city, you know that? Parties, friends…us," she says, emphasizing the last word. "I don't know what I'd have done without you."

"I don't think it would have been a problem."

"Not so sure about that, Donut Prince. I have a way of blowing up good things."

"Philly?"

She nods.

"Nothing to blow up here," I say playfully. "Just you and me—and my awesome jacket."

"I feel like I need an awesome jacket or something now," she says. "They close in twenty minutes. Do you mind if I look before we go?"

"Not a problem. I'm super comfortable in clothing stores."

She laughs. "Don't move."

In the pause, I stand in the glow of the overhead lights, watching the employees folding and cleaning the store before closing. I'm great for about ten seconds, and then the confusion sets in. What's going on between me and Daisy. Are we dating? Is she my girlfriend?

I'm starting to spin out when I hear Daisy's calling me.

"Can I get your opinion about something?" she asks.

I find her in the women's section. Before I can protest, she pulls me through the door into a dressing room and closes the door behind us.

"I need your honest opinion," she says, like this is an everyday event.

"Sure," I say, and she pulls her blouse over her head.

I stand there, dumbstruck, looking at her in a black lace bra, the swell of her breasts threatening to spill out of the cups.

"You need my opinion now, or—"

She grins and shakes her head. "After I put it on," she says.

I look down shyly.

"Don't look away," she says.

She arches her back and pulls a gray-ribbed turtleneck over her head. She frees her hair, briefly checks herself in the mirror, then turns back to me.

"What do you think for fall? Warm, comfy, but it's got swag."

"It looks great," I say.

"It's soft, too. Feel."

She holds out her arm, urging me to touch the fabric. I run my hand up her arm, and she places her hand over mine, slowly guiding it across her collarbone and onto her breast.

I sigh in pleasure. She watches me, gauging my reaction. We linger there, her hand holding mine against her breast, and then she slowly moves it up to her neck.

I lean in and we kiss, soft and slow, a kiss that leaves both of us breathless.

"Daisy—"

She puts a finger to my lips to quiet me.

"You don't have to hate shopping anymore," she says. "Next time you go to a store, you can forget about yourself—and remember me."

"I don't know what to say."

"Don't say anything." She smiles sweetly. "It's my birthday gift to you."

CHAPTER THIRTY-FIVE:
WORDS ON THE WIND

I stand in front of Manny Cruz's bench in Central Park, watching him play with his dog. Oso growls and make short order of a stick. When Manny sees me, he looks up and smiles, his gruff voice breaking me out of my trance.

"Eugene, seems like I haven't seen you in a long time. What brings you to my corner of the world?" he asks.

"Just out for a walk," I say.

I feel a little guilty that I haven't talked to Manny in a while. I've been busy with football and everything, but I realize I've also been avoiding him.

He wipes off the bench beside him and pats an empty spot. "How's the writing coming?"

I sigh and sit down hard. "It's good," I say.

"Unconvincing in the extreme," he says.

I reach over to pet Oso, but he growls a warning.

Manny takes a piece of bacon out of his pocket and hands it to me so I can give it to the little dog.

He looks at me, a knowing glint in his eye. "Why'd you stop writing?"

"I'm writing. Just… slowly."

Manny shakes his head. "I'm not buying it, brother. What's really going on?"

I hesitate, but I know Manny won't let up until I tell him the truth. "It's just… I've been spending more time with football. And girls."

"Girls plural?"

"A girl. Singular."

"Well now," Manny says with a lilt in his voice.

"How do you know when a girl is your girlfriend, Manny?"

"That's an interesting question," Manny says. "From my vast experience of dating dozens of beautiful women—"

"You've done that?" I ask excitedly.

"Not so much. You've heard of the play *A Few Good Men*?"

"Sure."

"My romantic memoir would be called *A Few Good Actresses*."

"That's a few more than I've dated," I say.

"I guess at some point a relationship crosses an invisible line, and you're either a couple or you're not."

"I'm confused by this girl. We had a date and it was amazing. She even bought me this jacket," I say, pointing to my new corduroy.

"There's something about a furry collar," Manny says.

"Right? But I never know when I'm going to see her again. Or if I'm going to see her. Does that make any sense?"

"It sounds like you want her to be your girlfriend."

I sit back on the bench, startled.

"Is that what it is?"

I imagine Daisy and me holding hands in the hallway, having lunch together, hanging out after football games. I can see it all so clearly, almost like a scene from a play being revealed in my mind.

"You're right," I say. "I want Daisy to be my girlfriend."

Manny looks on, pleased. "Then it's time to have an honest conversation. Tell her where you're at and ask her what she wants."

"Just come right out and ask?"

"Don't blurt it out when she's got a chicken tender in her mouth. Wait for the right moment. But when you feel that moment, lean in and pop the question."

An elderly couple passes by walking two poodles. One of the poodles sniffs its way toward Oso.

"Is he friendly?" the old woman asks.

"Not in the least," Manny says, and she quickly pulls the poodle back and hurries away with her husband.

Manny turns back to me. "So you're not writing. That's what you were telling me before."

"I'm not," I say, ashamed to admit the truth.

"I get it," Manny says.

"You're not angry at me?"

"Why would I be angry?"

"I just assumed—"

"*If you're not a writer, then what are you?* It's an important question to think about from time to time."

"If I'm not a writer?"

"It's supposed to be a passion, not a punishment. The way I see it, Eugene, words are a gift from the muse. If you don't want them, she'll give them to someone who does."

"What if I still want them?"

"Simple. Just get quiet and invite them in."

"I don't like getting quiet."

"Nobody does these days. That's why it's simple, but it ain't easy."

I sigh and lean back on the bench, and Manny does the same.

I look around the park and take it all in: the kaleidoscope of fall leaves, the music of the birdsongs, the chatter of people passing by, punctuated by the distant sound of cabs honking on the streets outside the park.

I feel New York all around me, and I suddenly remember what it's like to want to write. I imagine people watching plays I write, talking about my stories, arguing about their favorite characters. I think about the story I wanted to tell, an overweight character in an amazing love story.

I can almost hear the words of my next play, but they're so faint, I'm afraid to move and lose them.

Manny takes a long breath, and then he speaks, his voice just above a whisper.

"Can you hear them?"

I close my eyes.

"Yeah."

"Then it sounds like you've got some work to do," Manny says.

CHAPTER THIRTY-SIX:
THE END

When I get home, the conversation with Manny is lingering in my head. For the first time in a long time, I *feel* like writing. I'm even excited about it.

I sit at my desk and take out my writing notebook. I flip through a few pages, remembering where I left off the last time. But it's been so long, the work has grown cold, and I can barely remember what I was writing or why I wanted to write it.

I decide to do a writing prompt like Manny taught me last year. Manny said when you can't write what you want to write, write what someone else tells you to write.

So I pull out the list of prompts I have on my Apple notes.

A stranger comes up to you in a coffee shop and tells you there's an emergency and she needs your help. Write the dialogue as fast as you can:

I look at the blank page in front of me. The emptiness mocks me, daring me to fill it with words that actually mean something. Or don't.

Isn't the whole idea of a prompt not to think and just start your pen moving?

I try to make my pen move, but it won't.

I don't want to write bad words. I want to write great words. I want to be a famous playwright like Manny. If I can't be that, then why even bother?

So I put the prompt away, and I think about my new play.

SCENE 1.

A Sidewalk on the Upper West Side

MIA

It's our year to peak.

EUGENE

I'm more of a napper than a peaker.

I stop writing. It's too painful to think about Mia right now.

I reach for the donut holes and potato chips conveniently sitting on the side of my desk. These are the holes from Donut Prince that are like dense cake bombs going off in your mouth. Add in some double-baked chips, and I have my own private cafeteria. Mom doesn't need to know about it, and any evidence is smuggled out of my room and put in the trash chute before cleaning day. I probably shouldn't be eating instead of writing, but writers need energy, and these will boost my energy, right?

I taste the sweetness of the donut followed by the salt of the chip. I pull a chocolate donut hole apart with my fingers, place a layer of chips in between, and make a miniature donut sandwich. It's weird, but it's delicious.

No question I'm creative when it comes to food. Now I just have to apply that same creativity to my play. I turn back to the notebook.

ISHAAN

There's this girl you should meet.

EUGENE

Look at me, Ishaan. I'm not exactly dating material.

ISHAAN

Why not?

EUGENE

Because I ate a dozen cookies alone in my room last night.

ISHAAN

So we'll find you a girl who loves to bake.

I take a breath and settle into the chair. I make a mistake of looking down at my thighs. They're really wide. When I lean forward, they spread out and fill the whole chair. I suddenly realize I'm bigger than my chair, and I feel like a bear in a circus act sitting on a tiny little chair and typing while the children watch and laugh.

I prep another donut and chip sandwich and pop it in my mouth. Then I look back at my play.

No way. I'm not doing this.

I hate writing about myself.

Correction: I hate writing in general.

I see my name on Broadway, a brightly lit marquee above a theater entrance. And then, suddenly, the lights go out.

"Eugene! Dinner!"

Miriam Guterman, MD, beckons, my closed door no match for her piercing vocals.

"Be there in a second!" I shout back.

I have to hide the evidence of my snacks in case she walks into my room later. Donuts go into the box, chips in the bag, and both of them into my underwear drawer. It's not like the underwear drawer is guaranteed to stop Mom, but at least it's a deterrent. I wipe the crumbs from around my mouth and sweep off my shirt.

I look back at my writing notebook, open and barely touched on my desk. I need to hide the evidence of that, too. From myself.

I stuff it deep in a junk drawer, covering it with things I'll never look for or need.

I glance at my phone, where there's a long text chain with Wabash Simpson. It's a one-sided chain actually. For two weeks he's been asking about the play, asking me how I'm doing, asking if he can help or be my dramaturge.

I finally respond.

I'm not writing the play, I tell him. *Sorry*.

I immediately get back an emoji of a surprised face with an exploding brain.

I put down the phone.

Truth is, I'm not sure I want the words. If it was a choice between Daisy and words and I could only choose one, I'm pretty sure I'd pick Daisy. Maybe I already have.

CHAPTER THIRTY-SEVEN:
THIRD WHEEL FEELS

Dinner is depressing. It's not just the baked tofu and steamed spaghetti squash Mom cooked for us. It's me.

A few weeks ago my life was about writing and theater and hanging out with Mia and Ishaan. Now it's filled with Daisy or football bros—people I hardly understand and who I barely knew existed back then.

In the maze of my thoughts, one face stands out clearly: Mia's. We'd sit in diners, her doodling app ideas and me scribbling dialogue. Simple times.

I find myself outside her building before I even realize I've left mine. I even stopped at the corner to buy the chili mango chocolate bar she loves. The doorman recognizes me and waves me in.

Mrs. Kim opens the door, her face lighting up when she sees me.

"It's been too long," she says warmly. "Mia's working in the den."

I slip off my shoes and head for the den, my heart racing. I turn the corner, and there's Mia absorbed in her work on the sofa. A wash of relief sweeps over me—seeing her is like coming home.

I'm about to call her name when another guy beats me to it. He plops down next to her, perfectly at ease, like he's been doing it for years. *What's going on here?*

"What's up?" I say.

Mia looks over, startled. "Oh, hey. What are you doing here?"

"I was thinking about—anyway, your mom let me in," I say, feeling out of place.

She shrugs nonchalantly. "Okay."

I'm not thrilled by her reaction, but at least she didn't throw me out. After the fight we had a few weeks ago, I wasn't sure what to expect.

I gesture at the mystery guy.

"Oh, right," Mia says. "Eugene, meet Yujin. We're working on my start-up together."

Yujin… the name sounds like a variation of my own. I scrutinize the cool-looking Korean American guy, with his blue pants and untucked flannel shirt. He's total geek chic, a character from a Google intern poster.

He stands up and extends a hand. "Nice to meet you. Mia's mentioned you."

I skip the handshake and give him a half-hearted wave.

"Why are you acting weird?" Mia asks.

"I'm not acting weird," I say, even though what would you do if you were replaced by someone with a similar name?

"Are you guys working together, or what exactly?" I ask.

"Did you come here to apologize?" she says, her gaze intense.

A mix of feelings churns in my gut. "Yeah," I say, rubbing the back of my neck, searching for the right words. "I'm sorry for what I said after the game. I totally overreacted."

A genuine smile plays on Mia's lips. "Thanks," she says. "I'm sorry, too."

I hold out the chocolate bar. "Peace offering?"

"My favorite. Thanks."

She puts the chocolate bar on the table, then her attention shifts back to the laptop. "Come on in. We're getting ready for a Demo Day at school this weekend. Crunch time."

"What's a Demo Day?" I ask.

"It's a showcase," Yujin interjects. "You pitch your start-up, get feedback. There's even a prize for the best pitch."

"And potentially an invitation to State," Mia adds, her eyes bright with anticipation. "Actually, you could help. We need to make our pitch relatable. And you've always been great at telling stories."

That pang of insecurity hits again. I just quit writing the play to focus on football, and Mia dangles an opportunity. "I'm not sure I could write that," I admit.

Mia's gaze softens. "I think you could. Please?"

I glance at Yujin, and my heart sinks. Here I am, floundering about what I'm good for, and Mia's moved on, replaced our best friend duo with another Eugene. Thinner. Better dressed.

"Maybe tomorrow," I say as I take a step toward the hall.

Both Mia and Yujin look disappointed. "Seriously? We could really use your perspective," Mia says.

Yujin chimes in. "Come on, man. Lend us your writer's brain."

If I hear the word *writer* again, I'm going to snap.

"I'll see what I can do," I say, heading for the door. "Good luck with the cramming." I wave over my shoulder.

Mia, quick on her feet, follows me into the hall. "Eugene, are you okay?"

I chuckle, trying to deflect. "I'm fine. Just...figuring things out."

I notice her new look—the sweep of her bangs, the absence of glasses. "You've changed again," I say.

Her fingers touch her face like she's self-conscious. "Contacts. I thought they'd be more practical."

I smirk. "They look all right."

"What about you? Hipster jacket, jock buddies—"

I glance down at my jacket—and realize I've thrown on the corduroy Daisy bought me for my birthday. I pull it around me, suddenly uncomfortable.

"I guess we both moved on," I say.

We share a silent moment, suddenly at an uncharacteristic loss for words.

"The theater group misses you," Mia says quietly.

"I've been so busy," I say.

I start to feel guilty, and I do my best to push it away.

Mia sighs. "Just…think about helping us tomorrow?"

I nod, my throat tight. "I'll try."

She gives me a long look, then steps forward, wrapping me in a hug. The surprise and warmth of the gesture tugs at my heart. As she pulls away, her eyes search mine. "Take care, okay?"

"I will," I whisper back.

CHAPTER THIRTY-EIGHT:
MOVING ON

I walk home under an endless expanse of stars, feeling small and lost against the night sky. I cut through the park and end up stopping by the boat pond in Central Park. The thing with Mia shook me up. Every laugh, every shared look between her and Yujin keeps replaying in my head. I guess friends move on sometimes, even best friends. And her mention of the theater club?

Not what I needed tonight.

I'm not going to write, I'm not in the club, I'm not hanging out with Mia anymore, and Ishaan and I are friends but not best friends— That's a whole bunch of *not*.

I have to move on with my life. I'm going all in on football—and all in with Daisy. It's time for her to be my girlfriend.

I've never asked anyone to be my girlfriend before, and I could use some ideas. I whip out my phone and search for #promproposal. I'm not asking Daisy to prom, but it feels similar.

The search returns 339,000 results.

That's a little more inspiration than I was looking for.

I find an empty bench to sit on and I start scrolling, making sure nobody's around to see this embarrassing scrollathon.

My phone is flooded with high school romance clichés—great soundtracks, corny gestures, and over-the-top surprises. Straight proposals, LGBT, mixed-race, gender fluid—I see people being asked out in braille, in rose petals strewn down a hallway, in hearts mowed into a cornfield.

How many friggin' ways can you ask someone to prom? By the end, it feels like my head is going to explode, and I'm left with one lingering question— How have I made it to junior year without ever watching a prom proposal video?

If this is how kids ask each other to prom, I have to plan something unforgettable when I ask Daisy to be my girlfriend.

I figure maybe I could treat it like a play and write a speech where a character asks someone to be his girlfriend. Kind of ironic that I gave up writing a play, and now I need to write a play—part of one—to get a girlfriend. Only this time, writer's block isn't going to win.

I take a deep breath and head home. It's time to make it official with Daisy.

CHAPTER THIRTY-NINE:
SEAL THE DEAL

As I step into the school hall, Daisy appears, her eyes locking with mine. We both stop mid-step, the electricity obvious between us. At least I hope it is. *Is she feeling what I'm feeling?*

"Still recovering from our shopping adventure?" she asks playfully.

"You mean from my near-death experience in the dressing room?"

Her lips curve into a teasing smile. "I promise if you pass out, I'll come to the rescue with mouth-to-mouth."

She steps toward me, our lips dangerously close. "Maybe I should risk a trip to Old Navy next," I say.

Our private moment is cut short as a few soccer guys swagger by. One throws a flirty "What's up, beautiful?" to Daisy.

She laughs it off, but I feel a jab of insecurity.

"Friends of yours?" I ask, trying not to sound jealous.

She waves them off causally. "Just some soccer dudes. I don't really know them."

My stomach twists. "They seem to know you." Does being with Daisy mean constantly fighting off competition?

"A lot of people know me now," she says with a teasing smile. "Because I've been hanging out with a hot athlete."

"Which one?"

"I guess you'll have to figure that out," she says with a wink.

I rub my head, dizzy from the trip I just took from excitement, to jealousy, to pride, all in less than a minute.

"You okay?" she asks.

"Yeah, I'm just not used to—"

Dealing with women.

"Anyway, do you have plans tonight?" I say, recovering my composure.

"The plan is death by homework. I'll be in the apartment buried under a mountain of documents."

"Tough to breathe when you're buried. Give a shout if you need mouth-to-mouth."

She laughs. "You bet. What about you?"

"I'm supposed to help Mia and Yujin with something."

"Who's Yuj—"

"Complicated story," I say. "Let's save it for another time."

"Will do," she says with a smile. "You better text me later, mister."

"You know it," I say.

My breath catches in my throat as I watch her disappear down the hall.

If Daisy's going to be home studying tonight, then tonight's the night I ask.

No more waiting. It's time to seal the deal.

⊙ ⊙ ⊙

I'm stressed and excited the whole day, and it only gets worse after dark. I'm pacing in my bedroom practicing a dozen different ways to say what I want to say to Daisy, but the words are a jumbled mess.

It vaguely occurs to me that I should call someone for help, but who? I already talked to Manny, Ishaan has no experience with this, and Mia? I'm planning to ditch on her and Yujin to make this happen, so it's not like I can call and ask for her help.

I dig through my closet and pick out the best from my limited collection. My pants, once snug, now fit comfortably. I hate to admit that Mom's right—I'm losing weight. A small victory, but tonight, every bit of confidence counts. I put on the jacket Daisy bought me for my birthday, and I quickly check myself in the mirror.

The good feelings evaporate. I'm faced with the old enemy—doubt. I remember middle school dances when nobody wanted to dance with me, and my bar mitzvah when I outgrew my suit the week before services and we had to go to a tailor in the middle of the night to get it altered. I remember a group of kids in elementary school making elephant sounds when I walked down the hall. These and a thousand more.

My life as a fat kid, playing on a loop in my head.

I've never seen an overweight guy ask someone to be his girlfriend in a movie, or a play, or anywhere. Not unless it's some embarrassing comic relief moment. There are hardly any plays with overweight leads—*Hairspray* and *Dreamgirls* for women—and for men? I try to think of one, and I can't.

I look at myself, all dressed up and ready to go out, and I suddenly feel foolish.

My knees buckle as the courage drains from me.

I close my eyes tight, and I try to replace my bad memories with good. I think about my inspirational birthday with Daisy. And the night at the party before that. Then I imagine the nights to come.

So what if I've never seen an overweight character in a real love story? To hell with the traditional narratives and the stories *without* guys like me. It's time to write my own story. And live it. With Daisy.

⊙⊙⊙

I feel my anticipation growing as I head up Broadway. I'm a little troubled about blowing off Mia tonight. It sounded like she really wanted my help, but if I'm being honest—there's no way I want to spend time with her and Yujin. They were doing fine on their own, and I didn't outright agree to go over.

Anyway, it's now or never with Daisy. If I don't do it tonight, who knows when I'll get the courage again. I could be in college by then.

I'm a good ten blocks away from her apartment, just passing City Diner on Ninety-First Street, when a silhouette inside freezes me in my tracks. It's Daisy, engrossed in her iPad, sitting alone in a booth on the other side of the window, oblivious to the world outside. My internal countdown to prepare myself for our meetup goes to zero—she's right here.

Every rehearsed line, every draft of my speech vanishes. Forget doing it perfectly. All I really know is that I want her as my girlfriend. If I can tell her that, I'm sure things will be okay.

But as I'm about to tap on the window, her face lights up with a smile.

I track her gaze across the room, and I see Harry Habib coming out of the bathroom and walking toward her booth.

A flicker of recognition hits as I look back at her table.

Two glasses of water. Two place settings. Two forks. One big plate of fries in the center of the table.

To share.

This is no innocent study meetup. It's a date.

Harry slides into the booth, and the world narrows to the sight of him leaning in, their lips meeting in a kiss that seems to last an eternity.

Time stops. I feel every heartbeat, hear the clatter of dishes in the diner, the murmur of voices on the street behind me. A groan slips from my throat as I clutch my stomach, suddenly sick from what I'm seeing.

Harry and Daisy. They're together.

I can't believe it, even though the evidence is right in front of me. I look back at them wrapped in each other's arms like it's the most natural thing in the world.

I think of Daisy in the dressing room the night of my birthday, wrapped in my arms, kissing me, telling me how she felt about me—

Was she saying those things to Harry at the same time?

Daisy turns and her eyes suddenly find mine. Harry notices and he follows her gaze to me.

She opens her mouth like she's about to speak to me through the window—

I'm suddenly filled with rage. I want to shout, smash the window, confront them.

But I don't do any of those things.

I run.

I take off down the street as fast as I can, tears in my eyes, the city blurring around me.

I race down Broadway until I stumble, barely avoiding a fruit cart, and then I catch my breath and run some more.

Finally the weight of the moment—and my own body—slows me down. I push harder, trying to keep moving, but my legs give out, my lungs burning with pain.

I'm so angry I can barely breathe, and I can't get the image of Daisy and Harry out of my mind.

CHAPTER FORTY:
CLOSE YET FAR

In the moonlit haze of Sixty-Third Street, I clutch a bag of donuts, staring at the intermission crowd spilling out of Lincoln Center Theater. The buzz of the audience fills me with sadness. There was a time when I dreamt of being the name they'd applaud for—a playwright sensation. Instead, here I am, a jock reeling from a broken heart.

I take a bite of stale donut and angrily fling the remainder into an overflowing trash can. It's not the subpar donut that has me depressed—it's Daisy, and her betrayal.

I slump down on a bench and stare at the plaza across from me. This part of town used to feel so romantic—the fountain, the lights, the nearby park. But not tonight.

I hear the footsteps before I see him. It's Ishaan, hastily crossing the street toward me.

"I know things are bad when you're sitting in a traffic median," he says. He glances at the bag on my lap. "Drowning your sorrows in sugar?"

"Trying. It's hard with bad donuts."

"Is there such thing?"

"Once you've had Donut Prince, everything else is downhill."

He plants himself next to me. "Got your text. Spill."

I take a breath and recount what I saw at City Diner earlier.

Ishaan's eyes widen as he hears the story.

"Damn," he says. "What did you do?"

"I ran."

"Never run."

"It's not like it was a conscious choice. They were sharing French fries and saliva. What was I supposed to do? Stand there and applaud?"

"What would one of your characters do?"

"I don't write characters anymore."

"Oh, this is worse than I thought," Ishaan says with a heavy groan.

"I have to go back to school on Monday and see them both. Plus, there's a big game next week and I have to play with Harry."

Ishaan rests his arms on his head and takes a deep breath.

"Guys like us can't become guys like Harry," he says. "It doesn't happen. All that transformation stuff is good in a play, but it's not real."

I lean back with a deep sigh.

All my plans have failed. No question about that.

"So what do I do?"

"Stop trying." Ishaan lowers his voice. "When the play doesn't work out, maybe it's time to go off script."

"I'm not following."

"Have you ever thought of getting even?" he asks.

I laugh at the sheer audacity of the suggestion. "You serious?"

"Half serious," he says. "You got butt hurt. Maybe it's time to stop being the nice guy."

"Oh, okay. But kicking Harry's ass?"

"Not kicking it. Sabotaging it."

My chest tightens as I sit forward on the bench. "I can't believe we're even having—"

Ishaan interrupts. "You said you've got a game coming up, right?"

"We're playing Stuyvesant."

"What's your role on the team?"

"You mean position. I'm an offensive linebacker. I'm there to protect Harry."

He studies my face, waiting—

"I can't sabotage Harry," I say.

"You don't have to. I saw what you do in the game. You could maybe step aside on a play or two. Let nature take its course."

"I know what would happen. Stuyvesant would get through the line and Harry—"

"Yeah?" Ishaan asks innocently.

"He could get hurt," I say quietly.

"Accidentally," Ishaan adds. "Because you didn't do anything. You're the new guy and you just made a couple innocent mistakes, right?"

My mind is reeling. This is sounding like a full-blown plan from one of the nicest guys I know.

"I'm scared of this conversation," I admit.

"But it feels right, doesn't it?"

Suddenly, I remember Harry's party. Harry was making fun of Ishaan for flaming out with Jazmin before he left.

"You hate him, too," I say.

Ishaan's eyes flash.

"He hurt my best friend," Ishaan says. "Not more complicated than that."

"He hurt both of us," I say.

And Dillon. And who knows who else over the years?

"He acts like the hero but he has a dark side," I say. "I guess we all do."

"Payback," Ishaan says. "Food for thought."

"Bitter food," I say.

"Coffee's bitter, but people love it."

Silence stretches between us, broken only by the audience's return chime across the street at Lincoln Center.

I look back at the glowing theater lights, and I find my resolve.

"He never had my back, so why should I have his?"

Ishaan gives me a wordless nod. We both know what it means.

CHAPTER FORTY-ONE:
WHAT DID YOU DO?

I barely sleep all weekend because whenever I close my eyes, I'm looking in the window of City Diner. It plays over in a loop, a hundred variations of Harry and Daisy together, exploring each other's bodies, laughing at me, or sometimes ignoring me altogether like I'm invisible.

By the time morning comes, my heart is broken all over again.

All the time Daisy and I spent together, our late-night talks about life and love, her laugh, the things she whispered in my ear when we were making out—

Was she really doing all of that with me and seeing Harry, too?

She doesn't text me over the weekend. Maybe she's embarrassed or in shock, or maybe her fingers are too busy to reach for the phone.

How long has this thing with Harry been going on anyway? She challenged him to a race the first day of school and gave him her number. She said he never called, but now I wonder if that's true, or if she was just playing me.

I have no idea what's really going on and no way to find out. I just know I'm not texting her, but I keep checking my phone like a starving man studying a Grubhub menu.

I consider calling in sick for school Monday, but that's not going to change anything, so I show up. I drag myself through the day, wondering what I'll do if I run into her. Do you know what it's like to suddenly try to avoid the person you were always trying to find before? It's disorienting, like everything about school and my world flip-flopped overnight.

And then, it happens. I run into Daisy midway through the day, just after third period. I am walking down the hall to get to my AP English class, and she comes around the corner, approaching from the opposite direction. She looks up and our eyes meet briefly. I want to turn and run, but I already did that on Friday, and I'm not going to do it again.

So I suck it up and keep walking, doing my best impression of a guy who doesn't give a damn.

She puts her head down and I do the same, and we pass each other in the middle of the hall, both of us pretending we didn't see the other one.

Welcome to the last stage of high school dating. Post-romance avoidance.

Before I know it, the school day is over, and it's time for football practice. It's one thing to avoid a girl, but I can't avoid my own quarterback. We've got a big game at the end of the week, and we're expected to arrive at practice early and give 100 percent on the field. I'm not sure how I'm going to do that and not talk to Harry at the same time.

I'm heading to the locker room to change when I run into Dillon coming from the other direction. I hesitate at the door, waiting for him.

His face falls when he sees me. He must know something.

I motion silently, and I bring him around the corner so we won't be near the players heading into the locker room. I try to look at him, but he's afraid to meet my eye.

"What's happening between them?" I ask.

"What do you mean?" he says, feigning innocence.

"C'mon, Dillon. You're Harry's best friend."

"So?"

"I saw them together on a study date Friday night."

His shoulders slump. "I heard," he says quietly.

"So what's up?"

He crosses his arms and looks around, but it's just the two of us right now. Finally he answers me in hushed tones: "They've been hanging out for a while, Pudge."

"She's dating both of us at the same time?"

"Dating? I don't know if that's the word I'd put on it."

"Just be straight with me."

"I'm trying," he says. "Thing is, I didn't write the playbook."

"What's the playbook?"

"Harry's king of the castle," he says. "And the king takes what he wants."

His words hit me like a punch in the gut. Despite all my efforts to change this year, it came down to the same old truth.

I'm the fat guy—and Harry is Harry. And the Harrys of the world get the girl.

Dillon edges closer. "I don't know if it helps any, but you're not the first," he says. Something dark flickers across his face, and he turns and starts for the locker room.

I suddenly realize what he means. "What did you do?" I ask, and he stops mid-step.

"When?"

"When Harry did it to you."

Dillon sniffs once and stares at his feet.

"I moved on," he murmurs, and he rushes into the locker room.

CHAPTER FORTY-TWO:
GAME DAY

Harry and I don't talk during practice that day or for the rest of the week leading up to the Stuyvesant game. He acts like everything is the same, and so do I.

But nothing's the same, not really.

As I'm tying my cleats before practice one day, I overhear Harry on the phone, whispering and laughing.

Is he talking to Daisy?

My knuckles whiten as I pull my shoelaces. A coil of anger winds tight in my chest, combined with hurt and disbelief.

But I don't say anything.

During the week, I spend a lot of time thinking about my conversation with Ishaan on the median across from Lincoln Center.

And planning.

In those quiet moments, my mind replays my first meeting with Daisy, her hair framed by sunlight on the rooftop playing field, her laugh making my mood soar like a great musical ballad.

Then I think about Harry's betrayal—and what it would feel like to knock him down a few rungs on the ladder. Like Ishaan said, all I'd have to do is wait for the right moment in the game, then step aside and let it happen.

Some people would call that revenge, but others might say it's poetic justice. After what Daisy and Harry did to me, I think I deserve some justice.

⊙ ⊙ ⊙

As the bus rolls toward game day, an invisible line forms between me and Harry. He sits in the back on his king's throne, while I stay up front, as far away as possible. Even the other players sense it, keeping their distance like they're afraid to catch whatever bad blood flows between us.

The Stuyvesant game is downtown at East River Park today—between gorgeous views of the Williamsburg Bridge and the East River, and horrendous views of FDR Drive. The bus pulls in and parks, and Coach whistles for us to dismount.

I walk quickly away from the bus, headed toward our side of the field.

"Pudge!" Harry calls to me and beckons me back.

I steel myself and I reluctantly walk toward him. He casually steps away from the other players and I have no choice but to follow.

"We never got to talk," he says.

Right, because we've been avoiding each other all week.

"Talk about what?" I ask innocently.

"That night you ran off," he says, his tone friendly. "We wanted to talk to you about it."

"*We?* You mean you and Daisy?"

"Maybe, yeah. We discussed it."

"You're speaking for her now?"

"We thought it would be easier if it was one of us. We didn't want to gang up on you."

I shake my head. Not only is Daisy a liar, but she's also a coward.

I take a deep breath and look Harry in the eye. "So what do you want to tell me?"

"It wasn't what it looked like," Harry insists, his eyes avoiding mine.

In that moment, a memory flashes—Daisy saying I make her feel seen. Now Harry is doing his best to make me feel invisible.

"It looked like the two of you on a study date making out," I say.

"That's what it was," he says plainly. "But it was totally casual."

My teeth clench at the phrase. "That makes me feel so much better. See ya."

I turn back toward the field.

"Whoa there. You angry at me?"

"Yeah, Harry."

I turn back to see him bouncing from leg to leg, warming up while he's talking to me about destroying my relationship.

"Just remember it takes two," he says.

"For what?"

"To have a study date."

He grins smugly, like he just settled a debate. That really burns me up.

"So you're saying it's her fault? That's noble of you."

"There's no fault, Pudge. I'm saying you don't gotta be angry at me alone. Or at all. I'm your bro. And your QB. And your team captain. I wear a lot of hats, and also a helmet."

Is he trying to make a joke right now? I shake my head, disgusted by the conversation. If Harry had any idea of what I was thinking about doing during the game—

I turn away, afraid I'll say the wrong thing. I start toward the field, but I only make it about two steps before I whip back around.

I ran away once. I'm not doing it again.

"This was all about you, wasn't it?" I say angrily. "The party, the try-outs, Daisy."

His eyes widen in surprise.

"I didn't break my own wrist, Pudge. It wasn't some master plan. Besides, I never lied to you. I told you what I needed from you."

"You said you'd help me in exchange."

"I did help you."

"You helped ruin my life."

"What are you talking about?" he says incredulously. "Look at you. You're not the same person you were before. You're even up in my face right now. The shy geek I met a month ago wouldn't dare do that. How can you say I didn't give you anything?"

And right then, Coach walks over to hand Harry a piece of paper. "Congratulations," he says. "Some college scouts will be at today's game."

Harry's eyes go wide.

He turns to me, his voice cutting.

"Enough of this personal crap," he says, jabbing a finger in my face. "You got your little feelings hurt or whatever, but I'm playing out my season, you hear me?" His eyes flicker from the field back to me. "This is my dream and you're not gonna get in the way. So you'd better handle your business out there. Do you think you can do that?"

"Oh yeah," I say. "I can do it."

"Then man up and get on the field."

As he says it, I imagine a future of guys like Harry, taking the glory while I let it happen.

No more. It's time to take a stand.

⊙⊙⊙

My heart races as I step onto the field. This is only my third real game of the season. Above, the sky is bright and clear. The crowd cheers loudly to encourage us. I check the stands—down by center field, I spot Ishaan and a bunch of his orchestra friends who he brought to support me. They look extremely out of place, but they smile and wave, happy to have a new experience.

I look around for Mia. She hasn't spoken to me since I ditched on her and Yujin, so I don't expect her to come.

Still, I check. She's not here.

My eyes lock onto the VIP section. The college scouts are there, two guys in sport coats with notepads and serious expressions. They're not here for a game; they're here for the future—Harry's future.

The Upper West players tighten in for our first huddle, and I suddenly find myself thinking about my old theater rituals—prayers to Thespis and massage circles have become fist bumps and passing play strategy. I thought I'd let go of my theater roots completely, trading them for the football life. I was even starting to see these guys as a team and a family.

Now I don't know what they are.

Dillon and I trade looks, and I wonder what's really going on here. Is this a team, or a one-man show starring Harry?

As we lean into the huddle, I look over Harry's shoulder and see Daisy sitting down in front, watching us.

Harry's voice yanks me back to the huddle.

"Pudge! Head in the game!"

I glare at him and bite down on my mouth guard. In that instant, the crowd's roar and the thud of cleats on turf fade away.

Screw Harry. This isn't his stage anymore. It's mine.

Whistles blow, and we launch into the first quarter, the two teams evenly matched and fighting for every yard. Sweat is already pouring down my face as I collide with Stuyvesant's lineman without success. It's a deadlock, a tug-of-war with neither side giving an inch. Despite every ounce of muscle and strategy, the scoreboard remains a mockery: 0–0.

When the second quarter comes around, Harry calls a tricky sneak play. I can't help but be a part of it as Harry pretends to go back for a pass, but instead hands off to Langford, who runs it into the end zone.

We score on the play, but Stuyvesant bounces back fast, pulling together and driving downfield on their next possession to score their own touchdown.

Halftime arrives with the score tied at 7–7.

As the game plods on, it turns into the kind of event that critics—football critics at least—would call tedious. Incremental gains, botched passes, tackles that are more scuffle than spectacle. Every yard feels like a mile, every incomplete pass a missed opportunity that won't come back. I glance at Harry and see the frustration on his face—he's looking at the college scouts in the stands who he wants so desperately to impress—but I'm unmoved by his turmoil.

Finally, the fourth quarter arrives.

Harry gathers us for the first huddle, his eyes dilated with adrenaline. "This is our time!" he shouts, and he slams his fist into his chest, a call to war.

The team echoes him, pounding their chests and chanting, "Time! Time! Time!" to the point where even the Stuyvesant players start to look afraid.

It's my time, too, I think, pounding my chest with the others, my eyes narrowing.

My time to sabotage Harry—to let a Stuyvesant defenseman through, just for a second, long enough to take down Harry and end his glory days.

But as the ball is snapped and the linemen on either side crash into each other, I hesitate. My body goes into autopilot, defending the line, defending Harry.

We drive steadily downfield on our last chance to put points on the board and win the game. The safe play is to run out the clock, suck up all the time while getting ourselves within field goal distance. But Harry doesn't want an easy win. Not with scouts in the stands and a cast on his arm. He's got something to prove.

He goes for the touchdown. Three quick plays in succession, all of which fail. I do my job on all three, playing the good soldier, and laying down the blocks.

Pudge don't budge. Pudge holds the line. Pudge protects Harry at all costs.

Until we arrive at fourth and goal.

Last play, last chance.

I hear Coach shouting to go for a field goal, to play it safe, and I see Harry waving him off.

There's no glory in a field goal—not today—and not for Harry.

Instead, Harry calls the play, a pass/run option. He can throw it or drive it in himself, whichever opportunity presents itself.

Harry looks across the faces of the assembled players.

"We don't quit!" he shouts. "We finish the job!"

That earns him a roar of approval from the team.

It's the last play of the game, and my last chance for revenge.

There are so many ways I could do it. Slipping on loose turf so the Stuyvesant lineman races past and crashes into Harry. Missing a block, falling out of position as Stuyvesant pours over the line. Or just hitting at half-strength, allowing myself to be knocked down and run over.

I imagine Harry moaning on the ground in pain like he did that day in phys ed. I see Daisy crying, Coach screaming for an ambulance, the college scouts quietly slipping away.

All of that can happen if Pudge will budge. One time. Then everything else falls into place.

I set up on the line for the final play, and to my surprise, the flood of anger drains from me, replaced by something like pity.

Harry is human. He's fallible. As angry as I am, I get that now, all in a flash, like the inspiration for a new play about a beloved hero who is as weak as he is strong.

When the ball is snapped, I hold the line and push back, hard.

Pudge don't budge.

Not because Harry wants me to. Because I want to. For myself.

Suddenly I hear Harry's voice roaring behind me.

"Drop your head, Pudge!"

I follow his command instinctively, dropping my head and driving my shoulder into the lineman in front of me. In an instant, I feel the weight of Harry's hands gripping my shoulder pads, and his hard cleat digging into my back.

Harry is a mountain climber, pulling himself up my back, using me as a launchpad to hurl himself up into the air, somersaulting over the defensive line, and landing on his feet in the end zone.

TOUCHDOWN!

The crowd explodes with the loudest cheer I've ever heard. I let out a triumphant shout, my heart pounding in my chest. Harry and I lock eyes, then without a word, he pulls me into a bear hug. We've survived a battle neither of us expected to win. We dance in the end zone, surrounded by our teammates clapping us fiercely on the back, and the crowd on their feet around us, their shouts deafening in the crisp fall air.

In the eye of this celebratory hurricane, Harry grabs my helmet and yanks our faces so close I can see my own reflection in his eyes.

"This is us!" he shouts, his eyes sweeping to the pandemonium beyond. "I gave you this, Pudge. I gave you everything!"

Before I can even reply, our teammates sweep in, lifting Harry on their shoulders and carrying him off like a conquering hero.

CHAPTER FORTY-THREE:
THE AGONY OF DEFEAT

I stand in the middle of the locker room, surrounded by chaos and celebration. Everyone's cheering and congratulating each other on our big win. Even Coach catches the spirit, patting me and Harry on the back and telling us over and over what an amazing job we've done.

The guys on the team are partying all around us while Harry and I play the roles of conquering champions

Coach comes forward, taking me under one arm and Harry under the other, and he squeezes us tight.

"That was some next-level stuff," Coach says. "Teamwork makes the dream work."

"Sorry I didn't call for the field goal when you asked me to," Harry says.

"I didn't agree with the call," Coach says. "But you pulled it off. Double H to the rescue. And you, Pudge!"

"Me? I was just the human trampoline," I say.

"You were the trampoline when we needed one," Coach says. "And that made all the difference."

"Harry, did you tell him the good news?" Coach asks.

"Haven't had a chance," Harry replies.

"News?" I ask.

Harry grins and taps his orange cast. "The healing's been going well, so I'm getting this giant Cheeto off my arm next week. I'll be a fully functioning man again."

"Great," I say. I feel relief but also a pang of something else.

"That means you can retire now," Coach says with a smile.

"You're joking, right?"

"No joke. You're off the hook," Harry says.

"More like off the team," I say angrily.

Coach looks as me quizzically.

"I thought you'd be happy," he says. "No more sweating in the hot sun."

"But I like it," I say. "Or at least I don't hate it as much as I thought I would."

"That's not a ringing endorsement," Coach says.

"But I'm okay at it, right?"

"You're okay," Coach says. "You're even good. When Harry couldn't move so well, you kept him safe, but now that he's going to be back to full strength? Listen, you're coming to the game late, Pudge, and you don't have the training the other guys have. Or the agility. You know, because of your weight—"

And there it is. The truth.

My weight wasn't a problem when they wanted a wall in front of Harry, but now?

I'm too fat for football.

"You're going out on top," Harry says. "Not many people get to do that."

I glance around at the guys celebrating, and I want to be a part of them.

Coach and Harry watch me, their expressions blank.

"After everything I've done for the team, I don't get to decide whether I stay or go?" I ask. "That's it? I'm out?"

"You're not out," Coach says. "You can wear the uniform and ride the bench for the rest of the season."

"Consider it a victory lap," Harry says.

"Whose victory?" I say too loudly.

The celebration diminishes as players start to look at us.

"Why are you getting so upset?" Harry asks. "You never wanted to be a football player anyway."

"Says who?"

"Daisy told me."

"I don't believe you," I finally say.

"Facts, bro. She told me you were just playing football to get with her."

I go mute. Daisy talked about me behind my back and twisted the truth on top of it. Anger rushes through me.

"So you want me to sit on the bench," I snarl. "Like a mascot or something?"

"Whoa, that's heavy," Harry says.

"More like injured reserve," Coach says. "All of the privileges, none of the hard work. If you want, you can train with the team, get some exercise, keep up the good fight."

"The good fight?" I ask.

He glances down at my stomach.

Not that crap again. Why does it always come back to judging me by my waist size?

I bite my lower lip. I catch a glimpse of Dillon across the room. He looks at me sympathetically, but he's got no power here.

I'm alone in this.

"So what do you say?" Harry asks. "Are you ready for your victory lap?"

Harry holds out his hand for a bro clasp.

I can shake the king's hand, take the deal, wear the uniform for the rest of the season, save face, put it on my college record—

Screw that.

"You want a victory lap? Take one yourself. I didn't bust my butt to be a spectator."

The players in the room go silent.

I thrust my helmet toward Coach. "Find another mascot," I say. "I'm not your guy."

"Don't do this, Pudge!" Harry shouts, his voice cracking in disbelief.

I storm out of the locker room, bursting through the front doors, my plan of a subway escape already forming in my mind—

And I run smack into Daisy.

She's right there, ponytail and all, her face lit like she's waiting for her hero. The light dims when she sees it's just me.

"Hey," she says cautiously, like she's talking to a wounded animal. "I was waiting—"

"For Harry," I snap.

She opens her mouth, but no words come. In the silence, I hear everything.

I look toward the playground where children are playing, swooping down slides, climbing on monkey bars, screaming with joy.

"Congrats on your victory today," she finally says.

"Funny how victory doesn't always feel like winning."

I walk away. Then I get to the edge of the park and hesitate. I tell myself not to look back, unwilling to see the evidence of what I already know. But I can't help it, and I steal a glance.

A couple is walking arm in arm through the playground, clutching each other. Daisy and Harry, still together, the sun setting behind them, holding hands like the happiest couple on earth.

Two thoughts hit me at the same time.

I hate my life. And I want donuts.

CHAPTER FORTY-FOUR:
SUGAR HIGH

Days pass in a blur as the game fades to a bitter memory.

In school, I hold my head high and pretend I'm okay. To those who don't know me well, I seem like a winner, basking in the shadow of Harry's now-famous victory, the injured champion who overcame the odds.

But inside, I'm falling apart. My grades have slipped, and my writing notebook remains in the bottom of a drawer. I avoid Wabash and the theater club, dodge Mia, who still isn't talking to me, and occasionally hang out with Ishaan, where an ever-widening gap grows uncomfortably between us.

I eat my lunches alone and outside at my private wall, which has become all too private.

After school, I go to Donut Prince and drown my sorrows in flavor combinations. Sometimes I think I catch Daisy's reflection in the window, but when I look more closely, it's never her. It's some stranger in a leather jacket, just passing by.

And then, one drizzly weekend afternoon, I walk into Donut Prince and notice a flyer on the wall: "Upper West Theater Presents...A One-Act Play Festival." It looks like Wabash replaced my solo production with another festival. I can't blame him. I disappeared a month ago.

You belong with us, Guterman. That's what he said.

Now the festival is a week away. The theater club moved on, but I stayed the same. I guess Pudge really doesn't budge. I grab my donuts and crack open the bag, smelling the delicious, sweet aroma. On the way out of Donut Prince, I impulsively tear down the flyer. I'm about to throw it in the trash, but I stuff it into my pocket instead.

◎◎◎

I find myself walking back through Central Park. I sit on a bench and eat donuts out of the bag, one after the other, so fast that barely a crumb has time to fall. I shift positions and the crumpled flyer feels uncomfortable in my pocket. I pull it out, use it as a makeshift napkin, then toss it on the bench next to me. I pull my jacket tighter around me, bracing against the chill in the air. The ground is bright with Technicolor leaves, but inside my head there's only shades of gray.

"You beat me here today."

The voice pulls me down from my sugar high. It's Manny Cruz. Oso is by his side, sporting a turtleneck sweater that's a mini-me version of his owner's.

"Can I grab some bench?" Manny asks.

"Plenty of space," I say. "Extra donuts, too. But you gotta move fast."

He sits down and takes a bite of the offered donut. "These are incredible," he says.

"Donut Prince in Times Square. I have a frequent flier card," I say.

Manny sighs with pleasure and his eyes fall on the festival announcement between us.

"I've been wondering how it's going," he says. "Writing life?"

"I was supposed to write that full-length play, and I went MIA. They replaced me with this festival," I say, looking at the flyer again.

"The show must go on, right?"

"It went on without me."

"Yeah, that's generally how it works," he says with a knowing look. "If I remember correctly, last time I saw you, you were poised on the edge of a romance, ready to dive into life. How'd that work out?"

"It was a Shakespearean tragedy. I lost the girl, I'm off the team, my best friend Mia is now my ex–best friend, Ishaan is disappointed in me, and I let go of my theater dreams. I'm spiraling, Manny."

Manny nods slowly. "It sounds like you need an anchor in the storm, my friend."

"I get seasick on the Staten Island Ferry. I don't think I'll be dropping anchor anytime soon."

"I was talking about writing. The gift from the muse, remember?"

"Oh, the muse," I say. "I gave up on her a while ago."

A light rain starts to fall, but neither of us moves. Manny flips on a baseball cap while I pull up the hoodie I'm wearing under my jacket.

"Do you know why I started writing?" Manny asks.

"So you could be famous?"

"Overrated. I wrote because the world made no sense to me. Still doesn't."

"I'm not following."

He gestures at the dog owners in the park. "People, why they do what they do, the way they love and hurt each other—it's like a maze with no exit. When I write, I draw a little map for myself."

"Does it help?" I ask.

He pinches his thumb and index finger together so there's almost no space between them. "It gets me this much closer to understanding, and that's enough for me."

Manny gestures to the festival flyer. "This is your maze. And it's not too late to find your way through it."

"I can't write a play in a week," I say.

"I know playwrights who have rewritten entire scripts the night before opening," he says. "Though I don't recommend it. What were you working on when you stopped?"

"Mashups, fairy tales, parodies, and I tried…" I hesitate. "I tried a love story. It didn't work for me."

Manny gives me a knowing smile. "It sounds like life crashed into you pretty hard. Maybe that's your mashup—Eugene meets life."

"A love story about the three Fs—food, football, and failure."

"That sounds like the kernel of a play."

I take a deep breath and sit back. A wisp of an idea starts to form in my head.

I glance over to find Manny looking at me.

"Are the words coming back to you?"

"Maybe," I say.

Manny grins. "*Maybe* is a fine place to start," he says.

CHAPTER FORTY-FIVE:
THE PRINCE RETURNS

I sit down in front of my laptop, fingers hovering over the keyboard. I skipped the whole notebook and pen deal and went right for the big guns.

I take a deep breath and start to type. My idea for the play is simple. *Upper West Side Story.*

A boy named Pudge meets the girl of his dreams and his life gets complicated as he deals with new feelings about himself, his weight, and his body.

Pudge. I've been called versions of that name since I was a kid—fat, big, heavy, chubby, chunky, dumpy, Huge Teen instead of Eugene, and a million more—those names have always been a source of shame and insecurity for me.

When I joined the team, suddenly *Pudge* seemed like a good thing. A nickname with pride behind it. A chance to redefine myself.

But it was still other people deciding what they wanted to call me; I never got to decide what I want to call myself.

So Pudge is the name of the character in my play. How did Wabash describe it? "A contemporary twist on a classic love story that upends body image and gender tropes."

I'm not sure I know how to do that, but I'm willing to try.

I get quiet and listen for the muse.

Suddenly my fingers are flying across the keys. The outline flows out of me as I think about my life for the last month.

Before I know it, I'm ready to start my play. I open a new document on my laptop and I write the first line:

They call me Pudge.

I start to write about this character. He's more than just a football player, or a wannabe playwright, or his GPA, or his size.

I think about Daisy, all the things I wanted for us, and everything that didn't happen. Then I think about Mia. She was always there for me for the last five years, and how I ditched her as soon as there was something—or someone—I wanted more.

As I write, the maze of the story starts to come together, and I see my way through it piece by piece.

CHAPTER FORTY-SIX:
DEMO DAY

I look at the laptop on my desk. My play, *Upper West Side Story*, is on the screen. And it's finished.

I created a play, writing nonstop for an entire week, throwing everything I had into it.

What does Manny always tell me? *Finish a play, celebrate the day.* Now that there's a finished play in front of me, there are so many people I want to share it with.

Unfortunately, none of them are talking to me right now.

Mia more than anyone. In the past she'd read my plays before anyone else, before Ishaan even, and give me her feedback. Before our blowup, she'd been there all along, supporting me, encouraging me, pushing me to be better. She said it was our year to peak, and here I am peaking—not with football, Daisy, or the other stuff Mia never trusted—but in a way only she would get.

But I was a jerk, practically storming out of her apartment, then not showing up to help her and Yujin prep for Demo Day.

Since then I've dodged any communication with Mia, not wanting her to know how badly I'd messed up my life. But as I check my phone,

I find a week-old text inviting me to Demo Day. I was so busy writing, I missed the text.

But the Demo? It's happening today.

I transfer the play onto my phone and I rush out the door.

By the time I arrive at school the atmosphere in the auditorium is electric, charged with the collective ambition of every coder on stage. I slip into the back row of the auditorium, looking around at all the parents and students here to watch the presentations. On stage, there are rows of young coders, each group presenting in front of a panel of technologists who are critiquing the ideas and choosing a winner.

There are at least a dozen people on stage, but it's Mia who grabs my attention. She's just finishing her presentation with her coding buddy Yujin by her side.

She stands at the podium, looking really confident and passionate as she speaks about her start-up Anti-Social.

"There are serious problems with social media," she says. "Which is why Anti-Social is intended as a solution. The never-ending quest for approval from clicks, likes, and subscribes has to stop. With our site, users can connect in ways that are personal—they'll have full control over the content they see—and the content they show. Anti-Social is the end of FOMO. We want to give the power back to the people."

The audience cheers. Mia's mom is down front, clapping so furiously it looks like she's ready to jump onto the stage.

Mia and Yujin listen and respond as the technologists ask questions and make suggestions about the future direction of Anti-Social. By the time they step away from the podium, I'm convinced they're going to win.

Mia's brilliance shines, but it's not news to me. I remember her telling me about the idea on our walk, then sketching it out later in a notebook. It was so out there that I dismissed it, but Mia followed her vision, and now the world is finding out who she is. I could probably learn a lot from my friend.

My friend.

Mia was a friend and so much more. Advisor, supporter, and a great listener. She made me laugh and made me think. I miss walking with her every day, hearing about her world, and listening to her brilliant take on all things Guterman.

Suddenly I'm really sad. I'm jealous about Demo Day—I don't know anything about coding, and it's obvious she didn't need me to launch her start-up—

But she needed Yujin.

Is it possible I miss Mia so much because I have feelings for her? Not just friend feelings?

It hits me like a lightning bolt.

My feelings for Mia have been there for a long time, right in front of my face, but I totally missed them. I was too busy putting Mia in the friend zone, the same zone I was trying to get out of with Daisy.

Suddenly realizing you have feelings about your best friend is a lot to take, but before I can even figure out what I'm going to say to her, my gaze shifts back up on stage and skims over Yujin patting Mia gently on the back to congratulate her.

It could be an innocent gesture, but then their eyes lock, lingering a second too long. It's like they share a secret language, a secret world. One where I don't belong.

The end of the presentation seems to happen in slow motion. The technologists praise Anti-Social and declare it the winner of the event. The crowd erupts in applause, and Mia smiles like I've never seen her smile before, then Yujin gathers her in a triumphant hug.

It's obvious now. Mia and Yujin are more than friends.

I finally realized I have feelings for my best friend, but I realized it too late.

I drift toward the door. My hand hovers over the handle, torn between congratulating Mia and the reality crashing down on me. Finally, I slip the phone—with my new play—into my pocket and make a quiet exit. Mia has a new life now, and it's a life without me.

CHAPTER FORTY-SEVEN:
UPPER WEST SIDE STORIES

I stand in the back of the theater, watching my play come to life on stage. It's all thanks to Wabash. When I called him out of the blue, he welcomed me back into the festival with barely a week's notice. Now I'm watching my work being performed with a mix of excitement and nausea. The nausea is more prominent.

In the climactic scene of the play, the hero Pudge has to decide who to take to a party—Maizy or Dia. Maybe I could have stretched a little more when I chose the character names, but it is what it is.

MAIZY
> Make a choice, Pudge. You can't date both
> of us.

PUDGE
> Haven't you heard? "Throuple" is the new
> couple.

DIA (shakes her head)
> You have to decide who you want to be with.

PUDGE
> But I want it all.

MAIZY

    You don't get everything you want. That's

    not how the world works.

PUDGE

    I get all the donuts I want.

MAIZY

    And how's that working for you?

PUDGE

    Not great.

I scan the audience until I see Daisy watching from the back row. I wonder what she thinks about seeing an actor playing her on stage. I wrote the play hoping she'd be here and maybe think about me in a different light, but I just feel exposed with my story on stage.

I notice she's alone, no Harry in sight. Did they break up, or is it possible she just came to see my play? I'm embarrassed that some part of me still cares, even after everything that happened.

On the other side of the theater, Miriam Guterman, MD, watches the play with a shocked expression on her face. I don't think my mom knows half this stuff about me, but I guess after tonight she knows it all.

Mia, meanwhile, is noticeably absent. I recheck my messages to see if she got my text invite. She read it twenty-four hours ago, and she's still not here.

I try to refocus on the show. I've been watching the audience so much, I've practically missed the whole play.

The climax looms as the actor playing Pudge steps into the spotlight for his final scene with Dia. Dance music throbs in the background as the two of them are surrounded by actors dancing at a party.

The actor barely has time to say his first line when the lights flicker and die, plunging the stage into darkness. A murmur ripples through the audience, and my heart sinks.

Not now!

But then, as quickly as they went out, the lights flicker back to life. The actors are visibly shaken, but slowly the dancing starts again and Pudge pulls himself together and launches into the final scene, his voice stronger than before.

```
PUDGE (to the audience)
   Trying to hide my weight was like trying
   to hide sunshine with a donut hole. Good
   luck with that.
```

As Dia looks on, he awkwardly unbuttons his sweater and slips it off his shoulders, revealing his large stomach pressing against a tightly tucked shirt.

```
DIA
   What are you doing?
PUDGE
   What's it look like? I'm taking off my sweater.
DIA
   But you never take off your sweater. Espe-
   cially not at a party.
```

PUDGE

> I'm hot and I'm tired of hiding. So what
> if I'm heavier than most people? If every-
> one looked the same, the world would be a
> super boring place.

DIA

> Great. Then I'm taking off my sweater, too.

She does, revealing a beautiful blouse beneath. Pudge looks at her as if seeing her for the first time.

PUDGE

> You look amazing.

DIA

> Thanks for noticing.

Dia reaches out and Pudge takes her hand.

DIA

> Are you ready to party, Pudge?

PUDGE

> So ready.

PUDGE (to the audience)

> I've played a lot of different roles this
> year. I think I'll play myself now, and
> see how it goes.

Blackout. The lights fade up slowly as the cast returns to the stage for a curtain call.

The audience is silent for a few moments before breaking into a respectable applause. It's not the standing ovation I was hoping for, but it's also not the pained expressions and polite clapping I feared.

I glance at Wabash watching from backstage, his face filled with pride. He catches my eye and gives me a wink.

My new play isn't a failure; maybe it's even good.

I scan the crowd, and I can tell people are feeling it. They're still clapping, and my mother looks like she's crying, which I haven't seen her do since they discontinued her favorite kale salad from Peacefood Kitchen.

I only wish Mia had seen it, too.

Then a hand grips my shoulder. I turn to find Manny Cruz, my personal Yoda of playwriting, smiling at me.

"Were you hiding in the audience?" I ask, a little stunned.

Manny chuckles. "I'm allergic to audiences," he says. "Been backstage the whole time, right behind the props table."

"Wait, you saw the play?"

"Nice work," he says.

"I wrote it really fast. I mean, it probably could have used another draft."

He waves away the comment. "The fancy stuff comes later. You told the truth on stage. That takes guts."

"Damn, thanks, Manny. That means the world to me."

"Come by the park in a few days and we'll deep dive, bench-style."

"For sure. You want to come to the cast party?"

"Also allergic. I'll slink off to my uptown lair, but I'll catch you soon."

He salutes, then vanishes into the shadows at the back of the theater.

Manny Cruz, one of the best playwrights in New York, saw my play and didn't throw up after. That's not just a review, that's like winning a Tony Award.

CHAPTER FORTY-EIGHT:
TOO LITTLE, TOO LATE

The applause has faded, the congratulations have been doled out, and the theater slowly empties. The pre-show high becomes the post-show crash. Soon, it's just me and Miriam Guterman, MD. Her eyes glisten like she's struck emotional gold. I brace myself for what's to come.

"I owe you an apology," she says, surprising me.

"Hang on, I need evidence." I mime pulling out my phone. "Say that again, only slower."

"I'm serious, Eugene."

I put down my invisible phone. "Go on."

Mom's face softens. "I've been putting a lot of pressure on you. About your grades, med school—and your weight. And theater."

"It's a long list."

"I guess it is." She winces, then forces a smile. "Your play sort of made it obvious. I think I've been a taskmaster since the divorce."

"You said it, not me."

As if on cue, Wabash Simpson struts by, his head adorned with an illuminated hat that says "Another Opening" on the back and "Another Show" on the front.

"Is this your enchanting mother, Guterman?"

"It is," I say.

"It's great to meet you, Doctor," he says, and kisses my mom's hand. "And this son of yours—magnificent show, Guterman. I knew you had it in you."

"I'm glad one of us believed in me," I say with a laugh.

"I like your hat," Mom tells Wabash.

"Thank you. 'Twas a production unto itself." Then he bows deeply and walks away.

"He talks like he's seventy years old," Mom says.

"More like four hundred and seventy. It's kind of his thing. Anyway, did you really like the show?"

"It was beautiful. I saw a part of you I've never seen before."

"The writing part or the spilling my guts part?"

"All of it," she says. "Eugene, do you know why I'm not a fan of you doing theater?"

"You're afraid I'll be poor for the rest of my life?"

"That's part of it. But really—I don't want you to be disappointed."

"Why would I be disappointed?"

She takes a deep breath before answering. "Because your dad was," she says. "He wanted so badly to be a successful writer, and it broke his heart."

"I'm not him," I say.

Mom smiles sadly. "I see that now."

We stand for a moment, watching the stagehands sweep the space.

"You think you could lay off the medical school stuff?" I ask. "Even if I end up going, it's like half a decade away."

"You're right," she says. "No more body shaming either. Or whatever you call it."

"It's okay, Mom. I know you have my back."

She glances over my shoulder. "Looks like I'm not the only one who wants to talk to you."

I turn and see Daisy Luna waiting alone by the exit door.

"I'll see you at home," Mom whispers, and she gives me a quick peck on the cheek.

Daisy steps forward, a tentative smile on her lips.

"That was cute," she says. "Like a holiday card come to life."

It's the first time I've been this close to Daisy in a long time, and my emotions are swirling—anger, longing, sadness. It's like I've got an entire play going on in my head.

"You've got it all, huh? Football, academics, drama, romance."

I wince at the word *romance*. Daisy was my first real kiss. She's also the first girl who broke my heart. It's a little weird to hear her talking to me about romance.

"You know me," I say, trying to sound confident. "I'm a Renaissance man."

The line falls flat, even to my ears.

Our eyes meet briefly, and she looks away. "I wanted to talk to you without Harry around."

"Who's Harry?" I ask.

She attempts a smile and fails. "You really haven't heard?" she says. "We're done."

"You two aren't together anymore?"

"He's a player," she says. "And I fell for it."

"Join the club," I say, struggling to keep my voice even.

"It's painful, you know? Especially because I could have made a different choice."

"Different how?"

"You and me," she says.

"There is no you and me."

"But there could be. Again. If we both wanted it, right?"

My heart thunders in my chest as she steps close.

"Donut Prince," she whispers as her lips meet mine.

For a moment, it's like the epic climax of a movie. The smell of her skin, the minty freshness of her breath, the familiar feel of her body against mine—it's perfect in every way.

It should be the best kiss of my life. But it's not.

I pull back, confused. "I'm not feeling it," I say.

She looks shocked.

"You're not feeling me?" she asks.

I shake my head. "Not anymore."

She swallows hard, her voice coming in a whisper. "Then who?"

I don't answer. Her eyes search mine looking for something—anything—that might explain the moment.

"This has never happened to me before," she finally says.

"I guess you've done this a lot, huh?"

She shrugs. "I told you I'm complicated."

I clear my throat, unsure what to say. And then it comes to me.

"I gotta go," I tell her.

"Good luck," she says. "If you change your mind—"

I walk away without a word, each step taking me further from what could have been. I hit the door without hesitation, and I keep going.

CHAPTER FORTY-NINE:
THE GIRL OF MY DREAMS

Ishaan stands in the hall, eyes wide with surprise.

"What the hell was that?"

"Were you eavesdropping?" I ask.

"It was moral support from a distance. So what happened?"

"I told her the truth. I'm not into her anymore."

Ishaan shakes his head. "You're not into Daisy Luna, the girl of your dreams?"

"Interesting, huh?"

Ishaan looks stunned. "Here's what I don't understand," he says. "You got everything you wanted, right? Football fame, a great play in the festival, Daisy Luna—twice—so why do you look like you just dropped your iPhone in the toilet?"

I take a heavy breath. "All that stuff is okay, but big picture? It's not what I want."

Ishaan raises his eyebrows. "What do you want?"

"It's not a what. It's a *who*."

Ishaan's eyebrows shoot up. "A *who*?"

"Mia," I say, ripping off the Band-Aid.

"Anti-Social Mia?" Ishaan says. "Whoa, talk about a mic drop."

"Tell me about it."

"Does she know how you feel?" Ishaan asks.

"No." I shake my head. "But she needs to—ASAP."

"Well, that's a bummer," Ishaan says. "She left for New Haven with Yujin and the coders. They're going to the regional competition. She won't be back until Monday."

My heart sinks. "When did they leave?" I ask desperately.

"Sometime tonight. They're staying at a hotel—"

"A hotel?!" I practically shout, concerned by the thought of Mia alone with Yujin and all the things they might do together.

"Calm down, Romeo. A bunch of students and a chaperone. Nothing shady."

I pull out my phone and hit Mia on speed dial. Right to voicemail. Damn.

"Do you know what time they left?"

"I'm not her travel agent," Ishaan says. "But it was maybe an hour ago. From Moynihan Train Hall."

Moynihan Train Hall. I take off running.

"Promise you won't jump in front of a train to try to stop it!" Ishaan shouts after me.

"Now who's being dramatic?" I shout back, and I race into the street.

CHAPTER FIFTY:

IT WAS MIA

I barrel through the crowd at Moynihan Train Hall, my sneakers barely gripping the floor as I dodge late-night commuters like characters in a video game. My mind won't stop imagining Mia and Yujin in a hotel together, prepping for the competition late into the night, cementing their relationship into a forever plan.

My eyes dart to the glowing schedule high on the wall. New Haven. Platform three. Boarding.

Is it possible that's Mia's train?

Adrenaline surges as I race downstairs, sweat pouring out of me as I sprint for the platform. My eyes are on high alert, sweeping the crowd in a frantic search for Mia.

The train is still there, but the doors are already closed.

I drop my head in defeat. I missed her. I'm too late.

"Eugene!"

The voice spins me around. It's Mia standing near the one open train door, her face a mix of confusion and concern.

"Mia!" I rush toward her. It's the fastest sprint of my life.

I skid to a stop in front of Mia, gasping for breath.

"What are you doing here?" she asks.

I glance up at the train window, and I see Yujin's face pressed to it, his expression a cross between "lost puppy" and "jealous boyfriend."

"I had to find you before you left," I say. "I couldn't do this by text."

"Do what?"

She looks at me curiously, and I take a deep breath.

"It's hard to put into words," I say, my thoughts racing from excitement and lack of oxygen.

"Well, we've got like ninety seconds before the train leaves."

"Right," I say, launching in. "I always thought of you as a friend, right? Like a *best* friend, but still a friend."

"I thought of you as a friend, too," she says. "Until you turned into a jerk and ditched me."

"Sorry, I know that sucked. But my point is—what I realize now—you're more than just a friend."

"More how?"

I shuffle awkwardly. "I like you, Mia."

Her eyes widen in surprise. "You like me? Like, *like-like*?"

"That's a lot of likes," I say with a nervous laugh. "But, yeah."

"When did you figure that out?" she asks softly.

"When I saw you at the Demo Day. It was spectacular. You were everything up there."

"You were at the Demo? Why didn't you say hi?"

"I chickened out and ran for it. I watched your demo from the back of the auditorium, and it was like someone pressed the unmute button on my feelings. I didn't know what to do, but I didn't want to get in the way."

"Get in the way of what?" she asks.

I point toward the train where Yujin is still pressed against the window, his expression upgraded to a full scowl.

"Oh, wow," Mia says. Then she looks into my eyes. "You're sure about your feelings?"

"So sure," I say.

Her lips curl into a smile. "I feel the same way," she says. "Always have."

"Wait—for real?"

"Duh. We had our first kiss the summer after sixth grade, remember?"

I think about that late summer night after sixth grade when Mia and I admitted to each other that we'd never been kissed—then changed the story forever by sharing an awkward kiss together.

She never mentioned it again and neither did I, so I let it fade into history.

I've been so obsessed with firsts, I didn't think about the first I already had. Daisy wasn't my first kiss. Not really.

It was Mia.

"I guess I was embarrassed 'cause we were friends," I say. "So I kind of erased it from my mind."

"Not me. I caught feelings after that, Eugene. But I kept them to myself."

It suddenly makes sense why Mia wasn't on board when I fell for Daisy. She didn't want to lose me.

"I had to be okay with 'just friends' all these years," Mia says, "because I knew you weren't into me like that."

"How did you know if you never asked?"

"Because I know *you*. You like girls who get their nails done and stuff."

"And you like skinny, nerdy guys," I say.

I glance at Yujin, who is practically standing on his seat inside the train, gesturing for Mia to hurry.

"I'm definitely not skinny," I say.

"I know what you look like, Eugene. We've been friends for like six years."

"It's true," I say, and it goes quiet between us.

"Here we are," I say.

"Here we are." She hesitates for a moment, then she lowers her voice. "You know you're the only one who thinks about your weight like that," she says. "You look in the mirror and see someone who's not good enough. But that's not what I see."

I glance over Mia's shoulder and see a billboard ad for the Donut Prince, a giant maple-glazed donut glistening in the neon light. I've spent a lot of time with those donuts. Maybe too much time.

"What do you see when you look at me?" I ask Mia.

"I see Eugene Guterman. And I like him. *A lot.*"

"I want us to hang out, but I know I'm too late."

"Why are you too late?"

I glance back toward the train.

"Yujin? He's just a friend," Mia says.

"Friend with benefits?"

"The benefit is he's an amazing frontend software engineer."

"I don't think friends press their face to the train window like that."

Mia shrugs. "Maybe he likes me like that, but it's a one-way street."

"So can we do something when you get back from regionals?"

"Are you asking me on a date?"

"Definitely," I say, and Mia blushes.

"This is like a whole different side of you," she says awkwardly.

"It's the new me," I say. "I can dance, too."

She grins. "I'll be back on Monday. Maybe we could walk to school together for starters."

"That sounds great," I say.

She gives me a little wave as she gets on the train. It begins to pull away, the wheels groaning as it slowly gains speed.

Mia suddenly appears in the train window. She holds up a pinkie finger.

I hold up my pinkie finger, too, and Mia smiles.

This is our year, Eugene. That's what she said on the first day of school.

I think she was right.